The Shattered Glass
and
other stories from my life

Jasper Lal Chith

Life Stories from
a Rocket Scientist

BOOKSTHAKAM
TRANSCENDING BOUNDARIES

Published by Booksthakam, India
info@booksthakam.com
www.booksthakam.com

The Shattered Glass and other stories from my life : Life stories from a rocket scientist
A Booksthakam Book/ published by arrangement with the author

ISBN: 978-93-94378-82-7
Typeset and Cover Design by Cogitabund LLP
Printed and bounded in India by Manipal Technologies Limited

Table of Contents

To the memory of my parents
Grace and Chith Raja Dhas.
They gave their all.

Acknowledgement

I am indebted to Smt. Khyrunnisa, best-selling author and columnist for providing an insightful and precise foreword for this book. My grateful thanks to Dr Shashi Tharoor, author, international diplomat and parliamentarian for summing up and capturing the essence of my book in his inimitable style. I am grateful to eminent space scientist PadmaShri MC Dathan for encouraging me to go ahead with the book and for providing his insight on the book.

I express my sincere gratitude and appreciation to Shri Ashvin Raj and all my friends at Booksthakam.

Foreword

Nostalgia has its own special appeal. *The Shattered Glass and Other Stories from My Life*, a collection of short musings by Jasper Lal Chith, is an absorbing tribute to nostalgia. In these 30 autobiographical reflections, the author describes his experiences, either in the present or in the past, and uses the episodes to contemplate on the vagaries of life and the foibles of people.

An incident like finding an actual fly in the 'perfect 'cup of tea he had made makes him dwell upon some of the metaphorical flies in the soup or tea – minor annoyances - that he had met in his life. Watching children flying kites takes him back to his boyhood joys, and the kite's efforts to break free prompts him to philosophise on the fragility of human relationships. Losing and finding his house keys reminds him of symbolic keys like keys to happiness, good health or success, while the essay, 'Crossing the Line', describes the many kinds of literal and symbolic lines that one cannot cross.

A retiree from ISRO, the author is very conscious of advancing age, and in quite a few essays he dwells on that subject. A great desire to re-capture lost youth or pursue happiness made him a sucker for advertisement gimmicks that promised a thick crop of hair or a recipe to remain forever young – a dream rudely shattered when a man who was about ten years older than him addressed him as "uncle".

There is hilarity in 'The Family Doctor' and 'Marching with the Crowd', heart-tugging nostalgia in 'The Little Bird' and 'The Old Fool', self-deprecation in 'The Last Man in the Queue', 'The Con Man" and 'The Tug of War', an element of horror in 'The Bermuda Triangle in My Home,' and empathetic observations in 'Changing Times', 'How Are You?' , 'The Prisoner', 'Freedom at Last' , 'Angry Old Men' and 'I am a Hero Too.'

Written in an easy-flowing style, *The Shattered Glass and Other Stories from My Life*, with its deft blending of anecdotes and mild social criticism, is an enjoyable read. I wish Jasper Lal all the best.

KHYRUNNISA A

Author's Note

Our everyday life is made up of a series of events. Some of them are connected, many are unconnected. Some of these events may give us pleasure, some may make us unhappy. Most of these events are soon forgotten. But many which we think we have forgotten, have a way of resurfacing in our mind in some other context at a much later date. There is yet another type of event, an event which sets us thinking. Thinking about the foibles of the human race and the fallacies of life itself.

If there is one thing that I have learnt as a rocket scientist, it is to marvel at the wonders of everyday human life, the fragilities of human relations and human behaviour itself which are all far more complex than rocket science!

In my present book, I have attempted to reflect upon some of these events and observations from my own everyday life. Many of these events are from the recent past while some are from the long past. I am sure that most of these events ring familiar to you because they are all situations that all of us can identify with in our everyday life.

I do hope that you enjoy the book.

Here is wishing you all the very best.

Jasper Lal Chith

My Perfect Cup of Tea

I have no doubt that every one of you has made a cup of tea at one time or another. But, tell me, how was the taste? Did you honestly feel that it was as good as the super cup of tea that you took at the corner tea shop?

Well, coming to myself, let me admit that I am yet to master the art of making a perfect cup of tea. It seems to me that the more effort I put in, the less taste I get.

Finally, one day last week, I decided to take on the devil by his horn. From the internet, I downloaded the instructions for making the perfect cup of tea. I purchased a small packet of the costliest tea in the supermarket. I boiled the milk, added the correct amount of tea, a little bit of sugar and additional flavour. Now, the tea looked and smelt good.

Finally, here was my perfect cup of tea!

I poured the tea out into a beautiful china cup with a golden border. Now there was only one more thing to do: I like my tea at just the right temperature - not too hot. So what to do?

I switched on the fan over the dining table and placed the cup of tea directly below the fan. The fan would cool the tea in a short while. Then I arranged a chair for sitting and went to get the newspaper from the front porch – ***you see, most advertisements show the man reading a newspaper and***

sipping his tea. Once back inside, I took my tea from the dining table and seated myself.

Just as I was about to take my first sip, I was in for a shock. There was a fly floating in the tea. I recoiled in horror. My perfect, dream cup of tea was spoiled by a fly. I put away the cup in disgust.

Though the fly was dead, I cursed it roundly. Then I cursed the fan - probably the fan was the culprit. Gradually I calmed down. I realised that it was a case of the classical "fly in the soup" that originated in Greek mythology.

In Greek mythology, *before dying, the fly that fell into the hot soup is supposed to have meditated "I have eaten, I have drunk, I have taken a bath; if I die what do I care?"* ***I do not know what were the last thoughts of the fly that fell into my tea – I think, most likely, it cursed me for putting out the hot tea and switching on the fan!***

The Greek myth gradually transformed into an expression that basically meant a fly that fell into your soup either accidentally ***or was deliberately put into your soup / tea by someone else.***

Every day in our life, we come across instances wherein a fly is put into our cup of tea by someone, totally spoiling our tea.

I can give any number of instances from my own life. I still remember the occasion when I did an exceptionally good piece of work in my job; I worked day and night for two weeks and solved a very difficult technical problem. I wanted to brief my boss in person, but another co-worker, the "fly" in that instance, managed to brief the boss before I could.

I can give any number of light hearted instances too. I remember when I went to see a movie. My favourite heroine's movie had just been released. I stood in a queue in the hot sun for an hour (those days there was no online booking) and booked my ticket, choosing the best seat. When I went in, I purchased popcorn too. Just as the movie was about to start, ***the tallest man I had seen in my whole life*** entered and sat down in the seat just in front of me. I could hardly see the screen. When I summoned up courage and asked him if he would slightly shift, he flared up and informed me that he would sit as he pleased. Here was the proverbial fly in my tea! Another case was when I had gone to watch a thriller movie. Whenever thrilling action took place on the screen, the man next to me would get excited and shake his legs together, shaking my chair and a few other chairs which were all joined together at the bottom. When I requested him not to do it, he apologised sincerely. But during the next fight sequence, he got completely carried away again. He totally spoiled the movie for me. ***The number of instances wherein my cup of tea was spoiled by the proverbial fly cannot be counted.***

I have no doubt that each one of you can easily come up with a list of cases wherein your tea was spoiled by the same proverbial fly.

As I was brooding over this, I realised that the poor fly had had no intention at all to fall into my tea and spoil my morning. ***If I had only covered the tea properly, I could have still had my perfect cup of tea. Ultimately, the fault lay with me.***

Meanwhile, the morning sun had begun to climb. My family was about to wake up. What better way to get a kind word from my wife than to wake her up with a tasty cup of hot tea?

I decided to make two more cups of the super perfect tea, taking care that no fly fell into it this time.

The Clock on the Wall

When I was a young boy, we did not have a wall clock in our home. We only had what is known as a timepiece. The timepiece used to keep time for all our activities. Right early in the morning, the alarm in the timepiece would go off waking up the children and signalling a new day had begun. The mad rush in the morning hours was entirely centred around the timepiece.

Occasionally, the timepiece would strike work. Mostly, my mother would have forgotten to wind it up. What to do in the morning? How to know the time? Back then, neither of my parents had a wristwatch (wristwatches were luxury items those days and makes like Favre Leuba were everybody's envy). The nearest house was about a hundred metres away. Now, in that house, they had a beautiful wall clock. The clock was visible from the front, one could see the time by just standing in the street, near their front gate. So when our timepiece refused to show the time, it fell on me as the youngest member of our house to run up to the next house and check the time and report back to my mother. This used to happen quite often. Fed up of doing this errand, I used to pester my parents to buy a clock for our home too.

And then finally, one day, my father brought home a clock!

When the cover was opened, it was seen to be a gleaming, beautiful clock. It was of a rectangular shape with fine wooden borders. The clock dial was encased in polished glass. The pendulum part was covered by glass with exquisite designs. We debated where to put up the clock. It was agreed that it would be mounted in our main hall, on the wall facing the street, right in the centre. Then, it could be seen from the street too. The clock had a beautiful chime that was not quite loud. In the quiet of the night, one could lie awake and know the time just by listening.

The clocks in those days were all mechanical spring based types and had to be wound periodically. Our clock had to be wound once in two weeks. As the youngest in the house, it was my job to pull up a chair to the wall, stand on it and wind the clock. This was a difficult job actually - if I wound too tight, I risked damaging the spring. If I did not wind fully, the clock would stop soon. Gradually, I mastered the art of winding the clock.

Those days, we used to buy cow's milk supplied by some neighbours. Fed up of the high water content in the milk, my parents resolved to buy a cow. It so happened that around the time that we purchased the clock, we also bought a cow with a calf. To milk the cow, an old cow hand was arranged. When this old gentleman turned up early one morning, I saw that he was in his eighties, bent with age but still sprightly and moving fast with the aid of a walking stick. I went around helping him, carrying the milk pan and listening to his chattering. When he was about to leave, my mother told him to come early the next morning for milking the cow.

As I was escorting him out, my curiosity got the better of me; I asked him whether he had a clock in his home so that he could get up early in the morning and come. When he said he had no clock, I asked him how he knew the time then.

"Little boy" he said tapping his forehead, "my clock is right here."

So that is how he kept time. The next morning, he came pat on time too. So, this was how our ancestors kept time- by the passage of the sun and the length of the shadows and their internal clocks.

The years rolled by. We children grew up. Studies took us to other places. Our clock stayed at the same place. The years turned into decades. We children got married and had families of our own. Still, the faithful clock stayed at the same place keeping the time. My father now did the winding himself or whenever my sister or myself went to our home we did the winding. By now, all over the world, mechanical clocks have become out- dated and the digital and battery era has taken over. But still, our clock stayed on the same wall, faithfully keeping time.

When my father was quite into his later years, one day, he shared an incident from his childhood days. In his village, in the house of his cousin nearby, they purchased a beautiful wall clock. But nobody in that house knew how to wind it. So they arranged for a young man from nearby to periodically wind the clock. There was a beautiful young daughter in the house. On the pretext of winding the clock, the young man came frequently to the house. One day, the young woman was nowhere to be seen – a desperate search was launched; it turned out that the clock winding young man had run away with the fair maiden! This was a real life incident from my father's young days, which stayed in his mind and which he narrated to me after eighty years.

Our wall clock continued to occupy its place even in those later years. Occasionally, it had to be serviced. Even finding a suitable clock repair shop is so difficult now. But still, we kept it running. Sadly, one day recently, the nail on which the clock was mounted came loose, the clock fell down with a loud noise and broke. The glass got shattered too. There was no way that it could be repaired now.

None of us had the heart to dispose of our faithful clock. Now our wall clock is kept on the ground, leaning against the wall in a room, no more running, only resting.

Let it take all the rest it wants - after all, it had kept the time for us and kept us running all these decades, hadn't it?

The Mystery of the Shattered Glass

It was a night in the summer season a few years ago. I had finished all my chores for the day and went to bed early. Like the present summer, the weather was very hot at that time too. After trying to sleep for quite some time, I finally fell into a deep sleep. A deep, dreamless sleep.

All of a sudden, I woke up with a start. I woke up with the feeling that I heard a loud shattering sound - the sound of glass shattering. When I became fully awake, there was no sound at all, it was all quiet. But the ominous feeling of the sound of shattering glass still hung in the air heavily. My wife woke up too. But everything was quiet now.

What to do now? Of course, the first thing I did was to switch on the emergency master switch which immediately switched on the lights on the four sides of the house. I carefully peeped out through the window curtains- nothing moved, everything was still.

Now, should I take a torch and venture out? But I had seen too many videos on my mobile - videos wherein house owners were lured outside by a variety of means. One standard method involved opening the water tap and letting the water run, other methods involved taunting the dogs, throwing stones on the roof and so on. And my wife strongly insisted that I should not venture out.

So I decided not to venture out. After some time, I switched off the master lights. Now it was completely dark outside and absolutely quiet too; no noise of any kind.

No neighbour bothered to phone up - ***like all good neighbours, they made sure they were safe.*** Not even one neighbour put on his light, opened a window or made a simple phone call. This is the standard reaction one can expect from good neighbours in times of danger - they will lock themselves in and pretend they heard nothing.

Here all our good neighbours followed the standard protocol!

Tensed up and apprehensive, we stayed awake for some more time. Nothing happened further. Finally, we decided to go back to sleep. And sleep we did too, without any disturbance till the morning.

The first thing I do on getting up in the morning is to take my tablets, drink a glass of water and then put out the garbage bags. To put out the garbage bags, I have to come out of the house and open the gate.

On this day, I was especially anxious, fearful of what I would find when I came out.

As usual my car was still parked in the front of the house - I always park it in the open - but when I looked closely, I found that the window glass on the driver's side had been shattered. Splinters of the broken glass were lying by the side of the car and part of the glass was lying inside the car- glass fragments were lying right on the driver's seat too.

Otherwise, the car was untouched: the windshield and other windows were unscathed.

As I was surveying the scene, my good neighbours could no longer hold back their curiosity -now they not only ventured out but actually came to survey the scene.

They were quick to give out their opinions too!

One gentleman said it was a clear case of attempted car theft- that is why the thief broke open the driver's window. Another gentleman was more forthright - he said it was a clear warning to me - somebody had smashed the window as a clear threat and warning to me. Now, this was getting really scary. Yet another gentleman was sure that the rogues had actually wanted to smash the windshield but somehow missed the target and hit the driver's window. He was sure that the next time they would not miss.

You see, how nice, gentle and helpful my neighbours are?

Very soon, the police were informed. Two policemen came, inspected the car and made notes. They told me that I had to be available in the daytime when the forensic people came. On that day, there was the marriage of a close relative which we had planned to attend. But I could not go as I had to be available at home; my wife joined some other relatives to go for the marriage.

Many people came to know of the incident during the day. They phoned me during the day and offered me their expert views on what had happened –listening to all of them, the tension inside me began to build up. What should I do in the night? Whether the thieves or goons would come back again?

I am not sure whether I have told you earlier, but near my house, some people regularly dump garbage. The area is therefore home to a pack of stray dogs. These dogs can get ferocious at night. Nobody dared to walk in the area because of fear of the dogs. The dog pack would chase anyone who passed by on two wheelers too.

In this same area, we have a shopping complex which has an array of surveillance cameras covering various angles.

After the police forensic team left, I was pondering what to do. Suddenly, it occurred to me that I might get some information if I looked at the surveillance camera recordings from the shopping complex. I rushed to the complex. When I approached the manager who was well known to me with my request, he was immediately supportive. He took me to his recording room and together we went through the previous night's footage. Thus was the mystery of the shattered glass unravelled!

I knew the time that I woke up the previous night. So we rewound the camera footage to a few minutes before that time. The happenings were laid bare completely.

Five minutes before the incident, two young men on a motorcycle drove up the street, probably returning from a bar. They were not aware of our stray dog pack. All of a sudden, the dog pack appeared from the side chasing the young men on the bike. The dogs almost caught the young men who barely escaped.

But the young men were not ones to give up without a fight.

A few minutes later, these same men reappeared on the camera, but from the opposite side, now on foot. Both of them had big stones in their hands. The dog pack now scattered and ran down our street, the young men chasing them and throwing stones with full vigour. In the cameras, the dogs now ran past our house, the young men in full pursuit throwing stones. One of the stones completely missed its mark and shattered my car window; immediately the men stopped, turned back and ran. They got on their bike and fled. In a few moments, the cameras showed my house all lighting up - as I woke up and switched on the master lights!

As I watched the playback again and again and understood the sequence of events, a wave of relief swept over me. After all, it was neither thieves nor goons that shattered my car window - it was only the furious young men who chased the dogs and threw the stones, unfortunately missing their mark and shattering my window.

The camera recording was turned over to the police who completely agreed with the sequence of events.

Some of my good neighbours could not hide their disappointment at the turn of events!

No doubt they had been hoping for more excitement, that more action would happen on the following night and they could have fun.

Even though I was sorry to disappoint my good neighbours, I am sure that you as my close friends can imagine how relieved we were - that the mystery of the shattered glass was solved the way it was.

Breaking Free

Recently, some of our close friends visited us. They actually came all the way from the other end of the state. There were a few elders and two young children in the group. After an enjoyable day well spent, we took them to Kovalam beach in the evening. The children were happy and the elders were also delighted since none of them had been to the Kovalam beach before. Now they could go around in their village boasting that they had been to the world famous Kovalam beach.

At the beach, as we parked our vehicle and got out, we were accosted by the usual group of fancy goods sellers. But the children's attention was immediately caught by another sight – a few children running around on the beach flying kites. Our children immediately turned to the elders begging for kites.

No sooner had the children begged for kites than a kite seller himself arrived. He had with him a glittering array of kites. Bright red, green, orange, yellow - you name the colour and he had it.

The children were confused about which ones to buy but finally settled for two different colours –a bright orange and a bright red. The kite seller also provided a roll of string with each kite. Very soon, the children were happily running around on the beach flying their kites. The elders settled down chatting among themselves. My wife also joined them. In the serene pleasurable setting, slowly, the scene in front of me faded and I was transported to my childhood.

Among the happiest times of my childhood, any day, I would include the times I spent flying kites.

Every year, as soon as the summer vacation started, I would start making and flying kites. I made the body of the kite out of paper. The long tail also I made by cutting long stripes from newspapers and pasting them together.

Surrounding my house, we had a number of empty plots. The nearest house was quite far off. We had a beautiful breeze coming in because of the vast open space. To get the kite to fly, I would hold the kite and run a short distance. As the wind filled the kite, the kite climbed.

The kite took on a life of its own once it took to the air. It would tug at my hands asking me to release more string. The string had to be of good quality - should not be easily breakable and at the same time should unwind easily and should not be too thick either.

Gradually I mastered the art of making and flying kites. I learned that the kite needed a long tail for stability and that the tail should not break away during flight. So I made the tail out of light cotton cloth, the cloth from old torn sarees of my mother. After flying the kite for a few hours, when the time came to go home, I would reel in the kite. ***The kite would resist and tug at my hands trying to break free.*** But my strength would prevail, the string would hold and I would reel in the kite slowly and steadily.

Even as I was lost in these thoughts, I was suddenly brought to the present by loud noises.

I became aware of a young couple some distance away on the beach. They had been gesturing and talking animatedly. But now they were shouting at each other. They were not bothered about people watching them. Their fight went on vehemently. Perhaps their ***relationship was breaking up!*** Who cares in today's world anyway?

Talking of break-ups, recently I came across an incident which literally broke my heart. I was visiting my cousin in my home town. As I was walking along the street, I found a beautiful, well dressed and very distraught young woman standing in front of a house. The gate was locked from outside and apparently, no one was at home. I did not think much about it and continued on my way. After spending a few hours at my cousin's, on the way back, again I found the young woman still wandering the street in the same distraught condition.

As I turned the corner, I made enquiries with a shopkeeper whom I happened to know. What he told me was this: the young woman had been married to the son of that house. They had a child too. They were a happy couple and had been living abroad. Somehow, their relationship deteriorated. Maybe they both felt stifled in the marriage. Or perhaps it was an ego clash fuelled by interested relatives and others. In any case, ***they wanted to break free from the bondage of their marriage.*** Very soon, they separated and divorced. But strangely, they were still very fond of each other. Perhaps they thought it was all a big joke and that they would get back together again!

The young man soon came under intense pressure from his family to remarry. His parents soon found another girl for him and got him remarried. He went abroad again. His first wife came to know of this. From then on, every morning she would arrive at her ex-husband's house and wander around the street in a distraught condition. No one had the courage to approach her and talk to her. When I heard this story I was heartbroken. ***If only had they not broken free from the strings of their marriage! If only the string had held on for some more time!***

By now, the fighting couple on the beach had been separated by the onlookers. Both of them looked sullen. They would now go their separate ways!

I looked at the children. They were still flying their kites, the elders were still huddled together and I again went back to my reverie.

It was the last day of my summer vacation. I was flying my most beautiful kite that evening. I had an extra-long roll of string and let the kite fly far. I think the kite flew almost a kilometre away. Suddenly the sky darkened. Thunder showers were coming. I had to reel in the kite and run home. But as I tried to reel it in, the kite had other ideas.

At last, here was its chance to break free!

By now heavy drops of rain were falling. Urgently I tried to reel in the kite. The more I tried to reel it in, the more the kite tugged at my hand trying to break free.

And then in a flash, it broke free!

Perhaps it thought it could climb higher and higher and fly farther and farther away, but then it was actually falling away. Even today, I can see the kite falling away in my mind's eye. By now I was fully drenched and I ran home. I told my mother what had happened and she consoled me.

The next morning, I went in search of my kite. More than a kilometre from my house, near my school playground, there was a huge tamarind tree. Stuck on the top of this tree, I found the tattered remains of my kite, only the tail was still intact. It was so sad to see my glorious kite like that.

If only had it not broken away!

Suddenly I felt a tug at my hand. I looked down. One of the young children was wailing and pulling at my hand. "Uncle please help me, my kite has broken away."

I jumped out of my reverie and rushed in to help the child.

I am a Hero Too

The other day I was watching TV at home. The latest film hero was being interviewed. A handsome young man, his recent film had become a super hit. Everyone wanted to be seen with him. His haircut, mannerisms and dress style were the rage of the day.

My mind wandered over to the past.

I recalled the time when superstars like Rajesh Khanna and Amitabh Bachchan reigned supreme. Rajesh Khanna was in fact India's first superstar. Women swooned over him. His very appearance would send the women into frenzy. Nowadays there are heroes like superstar Shah Rukh Khan. In the western countries, it is the pop music stars who are the heroes.

Apart from stars of the entertainment industry, there are real life heroes from sports. Sachin Tendulkar, Neeraj Chopra and Sania Mirza are some of India's sports icons and heroes. There are other not so well known heroes from everyday life- those who toil for the welfare of the poor, those who take care of the suffering people, young people who show extraordinary bravery in the face of insurmountable obstacles and so on.

That brings me to the question- who is a hero? What are the characteristics of a hero? After pondering over the matter, I concluded - a hero is an idol. A hero is one who is admired and revered by others. They could never find a fault with him/her.

Every one of us would like to be a hero. How nice it would be to have other people admire us!

At least we would like to believe that we are somebody's hero. However, when I looked at myself and asked myself the question - am I a hero to anyone, anyone at all, sadly I had to admit that I am not a hero to anyone. They say that every man is a hero to his dog but I don't even have a dog. Thus, to put it bluntly, I am a hero to no one.

Gone are the days when a man was a hero in his home. In fact, nowadays, most women consider their husbands failures. For one thing, women excel in anything they do and they are better at it than men. In any case, whatever admiration they had for their husbands vanishes like a whiff of smoke after the initial phase of marriage. How about the children? Do they see the father as a hero? Many children do look upon their father as a hero during a passing phase of their childhood. That phase passes over, the scales fall from the eyes and he is no more a hero to his children.

So, is there anyone at all who considers an ordinary man a hero? Is there no one at all?

Are we really that unfortunate?

As I was brooding over this point, an old incident came to my mind. It happened more than forty years ago. I was standing inside a textile shop. A mother and her young son entered the shop and came over to the same counter. I could see that they were not well off economically. They were of average height; the young man was actually of less than average height. The mother wanted to buy a dhoti (veshti) for her son. As the salesman put out the clothes on the table, the mother insisted on seeing even more dhotis with more height, she kept saying,

"Show me dhotis with more height, ***look at my son, he is so tall."*** At that moment, a great truth dawned on me – ***to every mother, her son is the tallest, her child the greatest child in the whole world.***

It is this trait in mothers that produced Albert Einstein and Thomas Alva Edison. When the teachers told them that their children were no good, the mothers refused to believe it. To them, their child was the tallest. To them, their child was the most intelligent. And so it turned out to be!

You take the hardest criminal in the whole world, to his mother he is a hero and he could do no wrong.

In other words, every mother sees a hero in her child. To her, it doesn't matter if the child grows up to be successful or not in the eyes of the world. To her, her child would always be a hero.

When I realised this, I understood one thing – ***even the most ordinary human being is a hero to his or her mother.***

Yes, we can now rest assured that we are all heroes in the eyes of at least one person in the world.

Marching with the Crowd

Last week, the weatherman's prediction finally came true. During the past many weeks, the weatherman had been giving yellow and orange alerts for heavy rain every day; but the rain never came and most people had come to make light of the warnings. But last week, one day, as I was walking along the main road during the busy time of the day, suddenly the sky darkened. People on the roads scattered helter skelter looking for cover. Two wheeler riders hurriedly parked their vehicles on the roadsides and ran for shelter under the roofs of shops. I too joined them.

As the heavy rain started, it was an exhilarating feeling - watching the dark skies, the heavy drops of rain falling and people running to seek shelter. Even though I had an umbrella with me, I had not the heart to open it.

Very soon the rain stopped, the sky lightened and the crowds started to mill about on the pavements. I noticed that it was particularly crowded on the pavements and the traffic on the road was crawling. Apparently, there were quite a few protest marches planned that day - by students, by pensioners, by women's groups and so on. I walked along the crowded pavement enjoying the sights and the crowds.

As I was walking along, I became part of a group of young people, both boys and girls. The young people were chattering loudly and excitedly. I was so happy to be a part of this young group. The young people were all walking briskly and I was trying my best to walk along with them and to keep up with them. Since I had to walk fast in order to continue in the young group, I walked looking at the pavement carefully, so as not to trip and fall.

Suddenly, I heard slogans being shouted – I looked up and almost tripped and fell down in shock! The young people of my group were holding up banners and a party flag and some of them were raising slogans - they were actually part of a protest march.

Without my knowledge, I had joined a protest march!

Desperately, I looked for a way out. But the crowd carried me along; I struggled and with great difficulty and after a short distance, I was able to extricate myself from the group and the march.

My mind was in a whirl. Had anybody seen me marching with the protest group? I was not even aware of what they were marching for.

So this was what marching or flowing with the crowd meant? Is this what we call swimming with the tide? As I walked along, my mind was full of confused thoughts. It is so easy to follow the crowd, in fact, the crowd carries you along. We don't even have to think once we become part of the crowd. I realised that in almost all aspects of life we follow the crowd. It is not possible to go against the crowd. If you want to go against the crowd, then you lose the protection of the crowd and are exposed. It is so much easier ***and better*** in life to go along with the crowd - otherwise you could be isolated, ridiculed, humiliated and ostracised.

THE SHATTERED GLASS

An incident from my school days came to my mind. I think I was in the sixth or seventh standard. The science teacher was explaining the properties of water. He placed a glass tumbler on the table. Then he poured some water into it. Then he looked at the class and asked - if I tilt the glass what will happen to the top surface of the water? The crowd of students answered in a chorus: the top surface will tilt too. The teacher then asked a few individual students and they all agreed.

Somehow I felt otherwise. After all, it was water we were discussing and its top surface would maintain its level. When my turn came, I told the teacher what I thought.

The crowd of students stared at me in disbelief - what a fool this boy was! They all laughed at me and mocked me.

I had become an instant object of ridicule; all I had done was to go against the crowd.

When the teacher explained the answer and it became clear that I was correct, ***from an object of ridicule, instantly I became an object of hate!***

So this was what going against the crowd meant. I had learnt my lesson.

As I grew into an adult, I remembered the lesson learnt. Not for me going against the crowd. Not for me swimming against the tide. ***I always remembered that I am no one but a sheep in a herd.*** Wherever the herd goes I will follow the herd. If it meant that I had to close my eyes and ears when an innocent was hurt or when gross injustice took place, I would happily do that- otherwise, I would be ridiculed, hated and ostracised.

I was so caught up in these thoughts, I did not watch my steps. Suddenly, I realised that I was again going to become part of another group of people rushing to join the march.

JASPER LAL CHITH

As I broke away from the group, I decided to take another road, not the one in which the crowd travelled – but another one which was less travelled, one which was narrow, one which was uneven and full of stones, but one that would take me to my destination.

All is Forgiven

A few months ago, I had to visit a graveyard to pay my respects at the grave of a relative. That duty completed, I made my way back to the gate of the sprawling graveyard. As I slowly made my way between graves, I noticed that some of the graves were not well kept while some had polished tombstones and were well maintained. I kept reading the inscriptions on the tombstones of the departed as I moved along. As you know, usually the tombstones are inscribed with the names of the people and the dates of birth and death; a comforting verse from the Bible will also be usually inscribed. As I was moving towards the gate, I noticed one grave that particularly stood out; it was well polished and the black marble shone. I reached closer to that grave and read the inscription on the headstone; the man's name and dates of birth and death were given, but no Bible verse was given. ***However, in stark white letters on the black marble it was written: "All is forgiven."***

I slowly made my way to the gate and left the place. But the image of the inscription stayed in my mind.

Over the next few days, frequently I thought about that inscription.

Inscriptions on the tombstone are placed by the family, in this case, the wife and the children.

Why did they write "all is forgiven" on the grave?

Could they not forgive him when he was alive? What was there to forgive? Had he committed a crime of such a magnitude that they could not forgive him during his lifetime?

Perhaps during his lifetime he had not sought forgiveness and he had sought their forgiveness only during his last days; may be during the last days he was not in a position to receive or understand that he was forgiven. Maybe they wanted to forgive him, but could not bring themselves to forgive him when he was still alive.

Was the family trying to give him the comfort of forgiveness in death which they would not give him in life?

I realized that we will never know the true story behind that inscription. I wondered, ***is it possible to forgive at all?*** When I thought about it, I realised that a human heart can speak in different voices.

While one voice says forgive and forget, another voice says forgive but don't forget. Yet another voice says neither forgive nor forget, get revenge instead.

Is it really possible to forgive and forget? Personally, I think that it is not possible to forgive and forget when the heart has been wounded. I have noticed that people who claim to have forgiven and forgotten are able to vividly recollect the wounds (real or perceived) even after five decades down the line. They prefer to nurse their wounds within recesses deep inside their hearts. Then how can one claim to have forgiven and forgotten?

In many cultures, wounds are kept alive and passed down generations to avenge. As the saying goes, ***revenge is a tasty dish when eaten cold.***

After brooding over this issue for a few days I realised that the desire for revenge hurts the revenge seeker more as a festering wound. I came to the conclusion that it is always better to forgive if you can bring yourself to it. If not, at least keep all thoughts about it on the back burner.

As someone said, "Forgive others not because they deserve forgiveness, but because you deserve peace."

The Family Doctor

Gone are the days of the family doctor.

Long ago, during our childhood days, there used to be a family doctor for every family.

This doctor lived somewhere nearby. He would be accessible whenever needed. After trying out the country medicine prepared by your mother at home, if you still did not get well, then you would be taken to the family doctor.

In my case, our family doctor was an imposing man. He was nearly six feet tall and had a heavy build. While at home, he was usually dressed in a white banian with half sleeves and full length trousers. He wore a pair of thick spectacles too! But the thing that really frightened me most was his voice - it was booming and powerful and it was raspingly gruff too.

The greatest thing about my family doctor was that he knew everything. Many a time, he did not even need to examine the patient. All he needed was to listen to the symptoms and he would give the medicines. He had a medicine for every illness. And he mixed and made all the medicines himself, right in front of our eyes. There was a pink coloured liquid which he gave us every time for every illness. We had to take an ounce three times a day. Along with that, he would give large white coloured tablets. After going home, my parents would powder the tablet and place it on the tongue. It was so bitter. No amount of begging would help. Occasionally, they would take pity and give a little bit of sugar and some water.

Sometimes, the doctor would decide to give an injection. Oh no! As you know, in those days there was no disposable syringe. So he would sterilize the syringe in boiling water. He would go around the room picking up various things using forceps and immerse them in the boiling water. Finally, he would insert the syringe in place. All this would be done in full view. As he approached us to give the injection, we would beg him tearfully not to give an injection but to no avail- if he decided to give one, that was it!

The family doctor was also useful in another way to my parents. If we children did not take food properly, immediately we would be threatened with a visit to the doctor. Just thinking about his booming voice was enough to make me take my food. Now it so happened, that one day, it was my mother who fell sick. She had a severe cold. The usual country remedies did not work. My father was away at work during daytime. I was very young, maybe around seven years. In the evening, when I came back from school, my mother told me to go to the doctor and get her medicines. The doctor's house was quite close, so I could go and come safely. My mother clearly told me all her symptoms so that I could explain the same to the doctor and get the medicines.

And off I went.

When I reached the doctor's house, the doctor was at home. There was no other patient. He motioned me to sit in a chair. I sat down on the chair. Even though I was terrified, I was determined that my mother should get well fast. Hurriedly, I listed out all the symptoms. I made sure I did not miss anything. He hardly listened, all the time looking somewhat preoccupied. Finally, the doctor got up and went to his cupboard. He mixed his standard pink coloured concoction. Then he took a piece of paper, put some large white tablets and folded it.

Next, he took out his steel tray, filled it with water and put it for boiling. He carefully took his syringe and other accessories and put them too in the tray.

Why was he doing that, I wondered. There was no other patient present anyway.

Still, the light did not dawn on me. ***Only when he started walking towards me with the syringe did it dawn on me - the doctor thought that I was the patient***. He was going to give me an injection!

Terror filled me.

There was no time to lose. There was only one thing to do - run, run for my life.

I jumped up from the chair and ran. I did not bother to collect the medicines, I just ran. I did not look back at all. I stopped only when I reached my house.

I told my mother what had happened. ***It was not a laughing matter, but she burst out laughing!*** I don't know what was there to laugh about so much. I refused to go back to the doctor - no amount of threat and cajoling worked.

In the late evening when my father came back from work, he took me by hand and took me to the doctor. He explained to the doctor what had happened. They both had a hearty laugh. ***These grownups - would they ever understand the terror of a little child?***

Years rolled by. I grew into an adult. The doctor was now a white haired man.
One day, we happened to meet on the road. We politely enquired about each other's welfare. Then I brought up the incident that had taken place so long ago and ***we both burst out laughing!***

Forever Young

Recently I went shopping with my family in a big mall. As you know, these days a Mall is the place to be. You get everything under one roof. You get food, you get clothes, you get fashion items and you can even watch movies.

As my family got busy shopping, I was left with nothing to do. I decided to just loiter around. I decided to look at all the shops starting from one end. The shops were all beautifully and invitingly lit up. I decided not to enter any shop but just enjoy the sights from outside. As I was moving along, one shop in particular caught my attention. The name of the shop: "Forever Young."

What a beautiful name! I was just fascinated. Obviously, if you were young, then the products in the shop would keep you young forever and ever. I supposed the shop guaranteed that. But what if you were already old? Is there any hope for the old to get back the lost youth? The unfortunate old ones did not have the services of such a shop in their young days. But now that the products were in the market, could the old become young again?

Helping you to keep beautiful and maintain your youth is the job of big business. There are a number of ways to do that. One is obviously to maintain good health so that symptoms of old age can be delayed as far as possible. The other ways are to cover up old age by using cosmetics and personal care products, taking surgical interventions and ***taking medicines that guarantee to bring back your youth and vitality.*** The global yearly turnover of the beauty and personal care business alone is more than a whopping 550 billion US dollars!

Standing in front of the shop and watching the young and old alike entering the shop eagerly, I too was tempted to go in. But then, I remembered a story that I had read long ago - "*The Adventure of the Creeping Man*" from The Case Book of Sherlock Holmes. I think many of you might have read it too. ***A widower professor in his old age fell in love with his beautiful young assistant and wanted to marry her. Now obviously, he wanted his youth and vitality back.*** How to get them back? The professor, during his travels earlier had met a quack in Prague, who was in the business of selling products that made you young again.

Now, the professor got in touch with the quack in secret – and the quack supplied him with just the right medicine - essence made from black langur monkeys! This essence was guaranteed to bring back one's youth and vitality. The old professor started taking this miracle medicine in secret. This essence helped the venerable old man get back his vitality. ***There was only one catch- occasionally it made him walk on all fours and climb onto the terrace through the window creepers like monkeys did!*** So that was the price the old professor had to pay to remain "forever young".

Having read this story long ago, I decided to be careful. I decided not to enter the shop. I also decided to not approach any quack or even any local expert. Instead, like a wise old man, ***I decided to get advice from the internet itself.***

THE SHATTERED GLASS

The net was full of advice from the learned. After spending days sifting through them, I was able to arrive at the most important things to do to remain forever young: eat more and more fruits, do brain games (like Sudoku and chess - things that I never understood anyway), keep the company of the young, do meditation and get some exercise.

I decided to rigorously attempt to do all the above (I was ready to do anything in my desperate bid to get back my lost youth). I drew up a tight daily schedule and started off. Very soon, I must say that I began to feel younger and younger day by day.

All went on well till last week. What happened last week was this – I was attending a wedding reception, where, I met a man whom I thought was about ten years older than me; ***during our conversation, this man addressed me as uncle, that too in the presence of a beautiful young lady! Can you imagine?*** I was so disgusted and demoralised, I decided to completely give up my attempts to get back my youth.

I realised, that however hard I tried, there was a clock inside me beyond my control. I did not wind up this clock and I could never control the running of this clock. So I realised that we cannot remain forever young in our physique or even in our brain prowess.

Perhaps the only area where we can remain forever young is in our attitudes. ***I came to the conclusion that maybe by maintaining a refreshing attitude to youth and old age and ultimately to life itself, we can remain forever young.***

Crossing the Line

Recently an advertisement on TV caught my attention. It was for a product - for killing cockroaches. The product's name was Lakshman Rekha Chalk. All you had to do was to draw a line on the floor with this chalk and lo and behold, any cockroach would fall dead when it tried to cross this line.

This chalk was now supposed to be a woman's best friend. As you know, today's woman is bold and fearless. ***Very few things can scare a woman today and a cockroach is one of them.***

When I saw this advertisement and thought about it, ***I realised that even though there was only one line that a cockroach cannot cross, our lives are full of lines that we cannot or should not cross.***

There are lines on the road that one has to cross with caution. Whether you are walking or driving, you have to be careful not to cross some lines. If you are on a beach, there is a red line beyond which the sea may be deep and peril lurks. If you are trying to park your car in a busy area, then immediately you see a line beyond which there is no parking.

Recently, I was stopped short in a big office building by a warning - the board said, no entry beyond this line.

Even a ship has a line on its side, the Plimsoll Line. If you loaded a ship with more cargo such that this line went below water level, then God save the ship!

Then there are lines on the border between countries. You can attempt to cross these lines only at peril to your life. Of course, these lines may be covered by barbed wire fencing. Similarly, there is a border in the air called a country's airspace which coincides with the land border. In the sea, you have again an area beyond your land mass which you call your own.

There is yet another line which is also known as the borderline. A few years ago, my doctor asked me to check my blood sugar level. Dutifully, I went and checked in a laboratory near my home. When they gave me the result, I asked the lab technician about it - she said, "You are a border line case sir." What she apparently meant was, I could end up on either side later on, but presently I was on the correct side of the borderline.

Between political parties, there are dividing lines, defined over a long time but which are porous. There are a group of experts who sit on this border- they are called the fence sitters. At the shortest notice, they can jump onto either side from the fence!

But the most important lines are the invisible lines in our personal lives.

In every relationship, there are lines, invisible but clearly and strongly present.

We may not even speak about these lines but we know that we cannot cross the line if the relationship has to survive. In a family, there are lines which children cannot cross. For the parents there are another set of lines. A husband and wife relationship has a large number of invisible lines (landmines really!) .These lines develop over a period of time. Both the spouses know these lines are there even though they never laid these lines. If either spouse crosses these lines, the relationship will not be the same again – mind you, the relationship may be mended but will not be the same again.

Around each of us, we have a circle drawn by us which we call our own personal space. In a gathering or in a public place, we will not let anyone cross this line or space. We closely guard this personal space.

But coming back to the Lakshman Rekha Chalk.

I am really in a dilemma whether I should buy it or not. You see, I have a soft corner for the cockroach; after all, it could easily do what I never could - scare my wife!

Catching Spiderman

You have to give it to the newspapermen. They know how to catch your attention. Let me give you an example. Yesterday afternoon, I was just browsing through a local newspaper. I was in a lazy mood after lunch and browsing the paper made me sleepy. I was about to fall asleep when a heading on an inside page caught my attention. I shot bolt upright! In bold letters it was written "Spiderman Caught"!

I almost couldn't believe my eyes. How could Spiderman ever get caught? He is one of the greatest heroes ever. Not only that, he is also one of my favourite heroes. Let me be honest, I have seen all his movies and I love all of them (perhaps the last one was not as good as the earlier ones). How could such a superhero ever get caught? None of the great villains like the Green Goblin, Doctor Octopus or Sandman could come close to catching him. ***A silly thought flashed across my mind- was he caught in his own web?***

Hastily, I started reading; as I read the news, a wave of relief swept over me. It was nothing like what I had feared. All that had happened was this - the local police had caught a thief; this thief was popularly known as 'Spiderman Sabu' - you see, he could steal from any tall building. And like Spiderman, he could jump from one tall building to another! That is how he got his nickname. This pseudo Spiderman had a peculiarity -

even if the door of a flat that he was going to break in was open, he would not enter the flat through the open door; he would enter the flat only by breaking in through the windows. Such was his dedication to his art!

As you may know, before he became a superhero, Spiderman was just an ordinary teenager growing up in America. He lost both his parents at a young age and was brought up by an aunt and uncle and grew up into a troubled young man. ***Things were moving along without much excitement - till one day when he was bitten by a radioactive spider (whatever that may be!).*** After that, everything changed; he acquired superhuman powers: superhuman strength and agility, reflexes and intellect. He developed a web shooter in his wrist with which he could shoot webs over long distances. The web was so strong he could pull himself up at lightning speed and over tall skyscrapers. His girlfriend was the beautiful Mary Jane.

But coming back to the local Spiderman thief; this local Spiderman thief could easily jump from building to building. This reminded me of a great thief who lived in England in the eighteen hundreds. This thief was known as the jumping jack. He could jump over tall fences with ease, it was almost unbelievable. That is how he came to be known as the jumping jack! Nobody could understand how he did it. Finally, it turned out that he had fitted inside his shoes, special springs which helped him jump over fences.

While on the topic of Spiderman, have you ever wondered how spiders weave their web? Often when we walk through a door, or between plants in a garden, we walk across a spider web. But, how could the spider manage to put its web across a wide gap? Often, this web may be over a water body which the spider could not cross by crawling. Then how does the spider do it? Well, actually, the spider first produces a fine adhesive thread and allows it to drift on a faint breeze across a gap. It waits patiently for the thread to stick. When it sticks to a surface at the far end, the spider feels the change in the vibration. The spider then reels in and tightens the first strand, then carefully walks along it and strengthens it with a second thread. This process is repeated until the thread is strong enough to support the rest of the web. ***Incidentally, a spider thread is at least as strong as a steel thread of the same size.***

The persistence of spiders in weaving their web is well illustrated in the story of Scottish king Robert the Bruce. Bruce had been repeatedly defeated by his enemies. Finally, he was left with only a handful of men and he was in deep despair. At that time, while he was hiding in a cave, his attention was caught by a spider which was attempting to build a web. The spider failed in its attempts but it did not give up. It tried and tried and finally on its eighth attempt, it managed to build its web. Bruce took heart from this incident, rallied his troops and went on to defeat his enemies. He ruled Scotland from 1306 to 1329 AD and was one of its most successful rulers. ***All because he could take inspiration from a humble spider.***

But coming back to the news item. Relieved that only a local thief had been caught and safe in the knowledge that superhero Spiderman continued to fight the villains and safeguard the cities, I gave in to my urge for an afternoon nap. I fell into a deep sleep.

The Last Man in the Queue

Last Sunday, immediately after church, we went to visit some relatives. When we started back, it was quite late, in fact almost lunchtime. On the way, we passed one of the famous food outlets in the city. My wife suggested that we could buy our lunch from that outlet.

I agreed.

With great difficulty, I found a space to park and managed to squeeze my car in. Then I made my way into the shop. There was a good crowd milling around. No wonder. This outlet was renowned for the quality food they supplied. Quickly, I selected a few items for our lunch. Only then I found out that I had to join a queue to make the payment- the only way to buy my food was to stand in that queue. And to my chagrin, I found that the queue was long and that I was the last man in the queue.

As I stood in that queue cursing my fate, hunger began to gnaw at my stomach; it seemed to me that I was always the last man in any queue. No matter how long or short the queue and no matter how much I hurried to join a queue, I always ended up being the last man in any queue.

It was so unjust!

A number of incidents from the past flashed across my mind. There was an instance when I was at the railway reservation counter and as usual, I was the last man in the queue. The next counter was closed and therefore my queue was particularly long. I would have to stand in the queue for at least an hour. Just as I was resigning myself to my fate, there was a commotion in the front. Looking up, I saw that a lady had opened the next counter and was inviting people to come to that counter. Before I could make a dash, almost half the people in front of me jumped my queue and joined the new queue. It all happened so fast. The net result - even though a new queue formed, I was still the last man in my queue.

When I was in school, I happened to be the tallest in my class. Naturally, I always brought up the rear end in any queue or line which my class formed.

I passed out of school with good marks.

I decided to join a nearby college, a very prestigious institution. I went and got a set of admission forms from the college. I duly filled them all up. On the morning of the day informed, I reached the college along with my father. It was a prestigious institution and I found that there was a huge crowd of students and their parents.

Very soon, the staff asked the parents to stand aside and the students to form a queue.

Needless to say, I ended up being the last man in the queue!

Now there were only a few seats available in that institution and those in the line in front of me were going to be the lucky ones; time was running out for me.

Luckily for me, my father happened to know a staff member in the office. My father approached him and explained our plight telling him that even though I had very good marks, since I was the last in the queue I was about to lose my chance at admission. As soon as my father mentioned my marks, the staff member became alert. He came straight to me, took me by hand and led me inside the office. That is how I got admission into that institution in spite of being the last in the queue.

Coming to more recent times, only last month, I was waiting for check in at an airport counter. I had come quite early, anticipating a big crowd. I found that all the counters were open. Cleverly, I joined a queue that had only a few people.

For once I felt elated. Imagine my chagrin when I found a bunch of people, all pulling trolleys full of luggage join the man in front of me. It turned out that they were all members of the same family! Now when all the other queues moved, my queue remained stagnant and I was still the last man in the queue.

Often I have wondered - why is it that I am always the last man in the queue?

After pondering over this matter, I put the blame entirely on my parents.

*It was they who brought me up in **the foolish belief** that patience was a virtue.*

They told me, "Your turn will always come, be patient." But then, my poor parents were living in the past. They were behind the times, even in those days!

As all these thoughts were whirling through my mind, someone tapped my shoulder from behind. "Sir, please move". I came out of my reverie with a start. I had reached the sales counter.

I quickly paid my bill, collected my packet and left the store. As we reached home and partook of a perfect lunch, my mood mellowed; the ***realization dawned on me that the last man does become the first man in the queue when his turn comes.***

JASPER LAL CHITH

When I realized that, I did not feel so bad after all!

Angry Old Men

I am sure all of you know who the angry young man of Indian Cinema is. When Amitabh Bachchan burst on the scene in the super hit movie "Zanzeer" in 1973, India's angry young man was born. Many angry young men have appeared on the screen after Amitabh, but to date, Amitabh remains unequalled in his superstar status.

The angry young man in cinema always fights for the weak and the poor and always wins. While you might think that it is legitimate and acceptable for young men to be angry, what about old men? And I mean old men in real life not on the screen. Do you think it is legitimate and acceptable on the part of old men to be angry? Anyway, please listen to what I have to say and then you can decide.

One day last week, I was at home when my wife asked me to go and buy some household articles. Happy to be of some use, I got into my car and drove to the nearby supermarket. After finishing my purchase, I got back into my car, started the engine, turned into the main road and waited to get back into the traffic. I had to wait for quite some time before a break came in the traffic. Just as I was about to enter the traffic, an elderly man riding a scooter came at high speed. Even from a distance, the man looked very bulky. As he approached, I noticed that his mouth was red and full with chewing betel leaves. His helmet was loosely placed on his head. Just as he approached me, instead of slowing down, he began gesticulating with one hand. As he got still closer, he spat out the chewed betel leaves and shouted at me, abusing me loudly for daring to enter the traffic!

I was completely taken aback by his behaviour. As he passed me, I got a good look at him. I am sure the man was in his late eighties.

Here was a senior citizen, very elderly too - aggressively abusing me. It gave me quite a shock that such a senior man could be so aggressive and abusive.

Let me tell you another incident that happened in the same week. This time I was actually travelling in an auto rickshaw. The driver happened to be a very elderly man. He was wearing thick spectacles and his hands shivered. I felt quite sympathetic towards the man- after all, he had to drive an auto for his livelihood at his age. Just as I was about to start a conversation with him, a lorry got into the traffic in front of us. It was a narrow road and when the lorry suddenly pulled over to one side and stopped, we too were forced to stop behind it. Two labourers began to hastily unload some boxes from the lorry. They were aware that our auto was blocked and so they worked frantically. But my old driver was impatient. ***After a few minutes, he began to shout at and abuse the young labourers.***

These two incidents coming one after the other shook me up somewhat. ***I do not know why, but the abusive and nasty behaviour of the two elderly men greatly disturbed me.*** It was with a brooding mind that I went around.

The next day, I had to send a letter by speed post. Early in the morning itself I went to the post office. After getting the letter weighed, I went to the stamps counter and purchased the stamps. After pasting the stamps on the letter, I joined a queue that had formed in front of the speed post counter. It was a busy day and the queue was long. After a long time, I reached the counter. By this time, I noticed there was a long queue behind me too.

Just as I was talking to the man at the counter and was about to hand in my letter, came a young woman from the side, carrying a bundle of letters. She rudely pushed away my hand from the counter and pushed her bundle through the counter. I was totally taken aback. When I tried to protest, she turned loud and aggressive -"What is your problem man?" she shouted for everyone to hear. She looked so mean and aggressive, I had no doubt that she would have made a scene and faked a complaint against me alleging harassment, old though I was. The only thing for me to do was to stand aside. So she had her way while all the people in the queue waited patiently. ***Not one person in the queue had the courage to question the young woman.***

When I finally handed in my letter and went home, I was crestfallen.

The three incidents coming close one after the other completely shook me up. ***I had always believed that one should respect elders and women. But in a span of three days, my belief system had been demolished. I felt the whole world had turned upside down.***

Over the next few days, I kept turning over the matter in my mind. It has been always believed that the elderly and women were the weaker sections of society and they had to be respected and supported. But I am sure that you will agree with me that it was very difficult indeed to support the behaviour of any of the above three.

Why did the senior men lose their temper? Perhaps they were venting out their frustration in life. Perhaps there were many reasons for their frustration.

*There is no doubt at all, that, **as we get older, we realise that most dreams of our youth will only remain dreams - and there is nothing we can do about it.***

What about other reasons? In their own homes, the old are expected not to have any opinion of their own or even if they have –they are expected to keep their mouth shut. Occasionally, they are expected to be deaf too. ***Very often, the old are in desperate financial trouble.*** In addition, ***the aged have to deal with their physical fragilities too.*** Perhaps all these reasons caused the elders to vent their anger and frustration in my presence.

Do you now feel that it is justifiable for old men to be angry? Is it acceptable?

Well, in any case, the incidents with the angry old men taught me a lesson I will never forget- ***never take an elder for granted.***

Freedom at Last

One Sunday morning in the month of July, I was driving along the main road. It being a Sunday, the traffic was minimal and it was a leisurely drive. As I neared the public library, I noticed a large crowd on the side of the road. The crowd was in fact right in front of the library gate. As you know, there are many large trees in the library complex. I noticed that many in the crowd were pointing up to the treetops and gesturing animatedly. Curious to know what was going on, I pulled over to the side and got out of the car.

As luck would have it, I saw one of my old friends nearby, he too was looking up at the trees. I asked him what the matter was. He explained that there was a Hanuman monkey (gray langur) up on the trees. It was the same Hanuman monkey that had escaped from the city zoo a few weeks earlier, he explained. It had been sighted on the treetops in the library complex and the crowd had gathered.

I recalled reading about the monkey incident in the papers. A male Hanuman monkey (gray langur) had escaped from the city zoo a few weeks earlier. All attempts had been made by the zoo authority to capture it but to no avail. All sorts of enticements were offered. When enticements by means of fruits and food items failed, the authorities, it is believed fell back on the ultimate enticement- they brought in a female monkey. But even that could not make the male gray langur come down from the trees.

You see, once it tasted freedom, nothing else counted.

The monkey continued to roam about on the treetops of the city. It was occasionally sighted at various locations.

Sadly, about a month after the above incident, news came that the poor monkey had been trapped and caught. ***Apparently, the cunning and deceitful human mind had won again.***

If freedom was so important to a monkey, how about us humans?

Talking of freedom, many a time, every one of us feels the urge to get free, to "escape" from it all. But then responsibilities, attachments and fear hold us back.

Not so when it comes to teenagers. When I was in primary school, one of my cousins who was in high school felt the urge to be free. He quickly collected whatever money he could lay his hands on from home and took off. Remember, in those days there were neither mobiles, mobile towers nor CCTVs. Yet, he was caught and brought back in a couple of days. It came out later that he had apparently run out of money - ***but his steadfast policy in life was - "once a step taken forward, never a step backwards!"***(God bless his soul). So he had kept plodding on even after money ran out till his relatives caught up with him.

There was another incident when I was in my ninth standard. One of my classmates (in fact my late friend) did not turn up in school one day. It transpired later that he simply took off, nobody knew where. There was a frantic search. After a few days, he was brought back from Madras, apparently, he had the good sense to contact a relative when he ran out of money. It later turned out that even his father had done the same thing in his school days!

What is freedom and why does one need to escape? ***The need for freedom comes when there is a restraint - real or imaginary.***

The need for freedom is one of the most powerful urges in all living beings. We are all aware of the Berlin Wall that divided East and West Berlin. It was one of those walls that was supposedly impossible to cross. Yet, a few thousand people managed to cross over from East Berlin to the West. More than 200 people lost their lives attempting to cross the wall - mostly shot to death by East German border police.

Animals need freedom too. A tiger in the wild has a typical territory of 60 to 100 square km. How much territory does a tiger have in a zoo? It is typically kept in a cage of about 15 feet x 20 feet. Oh how generous humans are! What about little birds? We keep them in a cage in our front room after clipping their wings. ***And they hop around inside the cage singing their songs of anguish!***

There are many aspects in our lives wherein we need freedom. We need freedom in our homes, we need freedom of choice in everyday living and so on. In our personal lives, we need freedom within a marriage. When there is no freedom in a marriage, the marriage becomes a prison.

In our everyday life, we put on masks and assume roles.

These roles are thrust on us by society, by family and by our own individual needs.

There is no freedom. All our lives, we live yearning for freedom. ***As Jim Morrison said, "The most important kind of freedom is to be what you really are."***

The Hair Cutter

When I was a young man and till not too long ago, I had a good crop of hair on the top of my head. It was a regular practice for me to visit a saloon near my home once a month and get my hair trimmed.

Nowadays, age has taken its toll on my hair. I need to cut my hair only once in a few months. The hair has not only grown thinner, it grows very slowly too. So I need to visit the hair cutter only once in a few months. There is a hair dressing saloon near my house that used to be run by a father and son team. Even though there are many fancy hair dressing shops near my house, I still prefer this old fashioned shop - the father belonged to the old worldly school of barbers. He was a treasure trove of local news and gossip. He was also an expert on the latest movies.

Every time that I went to the shop, I would wait for him (the father) to get free and then insist that he only cut my hair. We would talk about the latest movies that were released. He could tell me confidently which movies were worth a watch. This continued for many years and over the years we became quite friendly. One day a few years ago, he told me he was going on a pilgrimage to Palani. Sadly, it was a pilgrimage from which he never came back. His son later told me that his father had fallen asleep on the bus on the way to Palani and had never woken up.

Nowadays the son runs the shop all by himself.

In the meantime, my hair has now become still thinner. The last time that I went to get my hair cut, I requested him (the son) to not trim my hair too much. The young man replied, "Definitely sir." Then he went on to mumble politely and in an undertone "There is nothing much to cut any way!"

That really upset me. All the more so because I knew he was correct. I did not say anything to him at that time, but I brooded over his statement for a few days. Finally, I decided to definitely do something about it. I decided to not only grow my hair back but also learn all about it.

Once I set forth in earnest, I learned some amazing things about our hair. I thought it worth sharing with you too.

There used to be an old saying that you cannot count the hairs on your head. That is no longer true. Nowadays, apparently, scientists have counted the number of hairs on your head. It turns out that an average person has about one lakh hairs on his head, typically varying from seventy thousand to one lakh fifty thousand. Of course, there are rare blessed individuals with a few lakhs of hair!

Many of us take very good care of our hair. If you do not know how to, all you need to do is to switch on your TV and the TV will tell you all about the latest hair care products. But however much you care for your hair, every day you will lose hair – on an average, everyday fifty to hundred hair fall out. That is because an individual hair has a lifetime – it can only live for two to seven years. Shocked? But don't worry – every day an equal number of hair grows back and thus your hair count is maintained!

Ever wonder how thick (or thin) a hair is? Well, a single hair is smaller than one tenth of a millimetre!

Interestingly both women and men have the same number of hair. Typically women keep their hair long but if they want, men can do it too. But most men begin their journey to baldness by the time they are thirty!

Typically hair grows at about ten mm (one cm) per month. As one grows older, both the rate of hair growth and hair regeneration fall drastically and whatever hair you have continues to fall at an increased rate! The net result is that hair becomes sparse and a visit to the haircutter becomes rare.

Of course in all the above, your genes play a part too.

I am reminded of a viral video that I saw recently. All of us will agree that Shashi Tharoor is one of the handsomest of men and an amazingly brilliant person too. You would have noticed that he has shiny long hair which keeps falling into his face and which he periodically throws back. The video showed him at an interaction with pretty young women. One young lady asked him how he could be so impossibly handsome and so charismatic at the same time. His brilliant tongue in cheek advice – ***choose your parents wisely!***

So friends, that perhaps may be the ultimate secret to a beautiful crop of hair!

The Musical Chair

Recently, I had an invitation to attend the inaugural function of an art exhibition. Even though I started well in time, I was caught in the city traffic and could reach only slightly late. The exhibition venue consisted of a hall with a front room. By the time I reached, I found the hall was fully packed.

The outer front room had a few empty seats still available. I occupied the seat closest to the hall so that I could watch the function. Just before the function started, one of my old friends entered the room. I had not seen him for years. I was tempted to go and meet him and sit along with him. But the fear of losing my chair kept me from getting up. I was sure that if I got up, someone else would occupy my chair. For a while, I was in a dilemma. Then, I decided to keep my chair. The friend could wait. Sometime later, an elderly lady entered the room, searching for a seat. I kept my eyes carefully averted. What if I had to give up my seat? Immediately after the inaugural function was over, I searched for my old friend, but he had already left. ***If only had I not clung on to my chair, I could have met my old friend.***

Last week, while travelling on a crowded bus, I was witness to a heated fight. One seat was about to fall vacant and two people made a claim for it. Here the fight was over a seat that was not yet vacant, but was only going to fall vacant as a passenger wanted to get down. The fight got so nasty, the other passengers and the conductor had to intervene and the bus had to be stopped for quite some time. ***All this because two people laid claim to a single seat which was yet to get vacant!***

There are different types of chairs that we fight over in our life.

A chair could mean a physical seat.

A chair could symbolically mean a lot of other things. A chair could be an object that we desire. A chair could be a house, a property, a job and so on.

Sometimes, a chair may be lying vacant and unclaimed for quite some time. But have you noticed? As soon as one person laid claim to it, many others would come forward with their own claims.

One business near my house was being run by the elder son of the family. It was a very successful business too. His two other siblings were living abroad. Recently, the father of the family passed away at a ripe old age. The other two children now laid claim to the chair, in this case the successful business! The siblings who were living abroad were especially particular that they should get the chair. Finally, the business itself had to be shut down, because not one of them was ready to let the other occupy the chair!

Often, a chair is a seat of power. Under the protection of a chair, one could do a lot of things including any amount of misdeeds. If you had to vacate the chair, you might have to pay a price for your misdeeds. That is one reason why people cling on to their chairs of power.

I still cannot understand what makes human beings so much attached to a chair that we fight for a chair as if our lives depend on it. Not for a moment do we think that we cannot hold a chair for ever. ***We behave as if a chair is meant for us and as if we will hold that chair forever.***

A few days ago, I decided to go for a walk in the evening. The best place to go is of course the museum grounds. As you know, there is a radio with a loudspeaker on the grounds and in the evening you can listen to it sitting on the benches in the area. Now these benches are all hard wooden types or made of metal with backrests. Each of these long benches can comfortably seat about four people.

Once I reached the museum grounds, I walked around for some time and then I decided to take a seat on a bench and listen to the songs being played on the radio. When I took a turn and went to the benches, believe me, each of the ten benches were occupied. How were they occupied?

On seven of the ten benches, one person was sitting in the middle of the bench, with both arms spread out fully covering the entire bench! On two benches, a man was lying down full length on each one! Of course they were all awake. In the remaining one bench, a young couple was attempting to spend some private time.

Determined to get a seat, I made two rounds of the benches deliberately slowing down in front of each (I did not disturb the poor young couple). ***I made it clear that I wanted a seat, though not in words.*** Not one gentleman moved a finger! They all stared right through me. It was as if I didn't exist for them!

Disgusted and dejected, I moved away looking for other seats. Why was it that not one of them was willing to make a minor adjustment? They were all educated after all.

Did they think that I would invade their privacy in a public place?

Did they think that they could occupy that bench every day and forever?
I admit that I am not able to explain human behaviour at all.
Ultimately, we have to accept that life is a musical chair.
So the chair that we cling to has to change hands. The chair may be a job, beauty, youth, a house, a property etc. But we get to occupy that chair for a very short time only.
After all, in the scale of cosmic time, the lifespan of a human is but a fleeting second!

The Little Bird

When I was growing up, we had a large front yard in our house. My mother was very fond of flowering plants. She used to plant different varieties of flowering plants in the front yard. Near the front entrance door of our house was a Jasmine plant. This plant was lush with leaves and flowers and my mother provided ropes for the creepers to climb onto the roof top. So you could say that a good portion of the front of our house was covered by the Jasmine plant. In the blooming season, the glorious flowers would cover the front wall of the house and part of the front yard was carpeted by the fallen Jasmine flowers. The gentle smell of Jasmine flowers welcomed visitors to our home.

Right in the middle of this plant, a little bird decided to build its nest!

I never knew when the bird started to build its nest; it must have been quite some days earlier. I came to know of the nest only from the bird's constant chirping. The bird brought twigs and dry leaves and darted about the Jasmine plant; the nest began to take shape. Now the bird constantly hovered around the nest, chirping and singing. She was a lovely little bird too, small and her colour was a shiny greenish blue. She had a beautiful tuft of feathers on the top of her head. Very soon, she laid her eggs into the nest. When the bird was not in the nest, I would stand on my toes and peep into the nest. There were three little eggs, cream coloured and with black spots. My full time job now became watching the bird, apart from going to school.

I was so excited, I told a few of my close friends too.

Now this nest was very close to our front door and could be seen by anybody if they noticed the little bird's singing. This gave me cause for worry. You see, even in those days, people used to keep birds as pets - inside small cages. ***Sometimes, they would cut off the wings of the poor little birds to prevent them from flying away. So the poor little birds would hop around inside the small cage and spend their whole life longing to fly outside.***

Oh! how the birds suffered! What is life to a little bird if you take away its freedom to fly?

Coming back to my little bird, I was getting increasingly afraid for the little bird and its nest, that someone might discover the nest and take it away.

It so happened, that, in my school, there were a number of older boys, bully types who made extra income by catching and selling birds. They would use the money to buy cigarettes and paan. One of these boys happened to live in our neighbourhood.

One evening, someone called out my name from outside my home. When I came outside, whom do I find but the local bully boy! The bully boy came straight to the point; "Is there a bird's nest in your house?" he asked. I was so scared for the bird, that I immediately blurted out an emphatic no! In my childish innocence, I hoped that the bully boy would take my words at face value. I could not realize that word had already reached him about our little bird from my schoolmates. He could see the nest too on the jasmine plant, right next to the front door. He gave me a strange look, "I see," he said and went away.

A few days later, one early morning while we were waking up, there was a strange sound from the front of the house. The little bird cried out in alarm and the sound of footsteps running was heard. By the time we came out of the house, nobody could be seen. I immediately looked for the bird's nest. Alas! it was not there. As we searched around the house we found the nest lying near the left side boundary wall (which was quite low) – the nest was empty. Apparently, the bully boy had pocketed the eggs, thrown away the nest and jumped over the wall.

I was heartbroken. I cried the whole day and night. My parents tried to console me - it was not my fault really, there was nothing more that I could have done and so on. But I was inconsolable- the bully boy would have come to know of the bird from my friends. If only had I kept my mouth shut!

The Little bird never came back again.

Poor little bird, it had trusted us and built its nest right next to our front door. Perhaps, in its innocence, it thought that was the safest place.

But we humans had yet again betrayed the trust reposed in us – in this case by the little bird.

I could only hang my head in shame as I shed tears.

The Lost Key

Many years ago, when my children were toddlers, we used to drop them off at the house of a close relative on the way to work. Both I and my wife were working in those days. In the evening, on the way back from work, we would pick up the children and go home. The morning hours were especially hectic, the toddlers had to be got ready, we ourselves had to get ready, the house had to be locked and so on.

One rainy day morning we were running late and we were in a great hurry. Somehow, finally, we got ready and I locked the doors. Frantically, my family got into the car and while helping them into the car, I kept the main bunch of house keys on the top of the car. Then I also got into the car and we drove off. We dropped off the children at our relative's place and then reached our workplace.

Sometime during the day I realised that the house key bunch was missing. Frantically I phoned my wife but she had no clue. I informed my boss and got permission to go home. I reached my home and retraced the entire path of my morning travel. The keys were nowhere to be seen. I asked all and sundry on the roadside if they had seen a bunch of keys. What added to my desperation was the fact that there were no spare keys.

Finally, with no other option left, I went to the nearest police station and met the station in charge. ***He listened to my story***

and then asked me what kind of a fool I was! I could only mumble something in response. ***He was entirely correct of course.***

Finally, he asked me to give the complaint in writing. As I was writing down the complaint, he received a phone call. After talking for a while, he put down the phone and came over to me. He said I was a lucky man; the phone call was from a newspaper office. Someone had handed over a bunch of keys at the newspaper office.

I thanked him and immediately rushed off to the newspaper office. In short, what had happened was this: the bunch of keys had fallen off from the top of the car onto the road when I drove over a bump. A schoolboy found them on the road, took them and handed them over to his teacher. The teacher informed the principal and the school arranged to hand it over to the newspaper office. That was how I got back my keys. I profusely thanked the newspaper people, drove all the way to the school, met the principal and thanked him; I met the student too and thanked him for his wonderful deed.

Afterwards, I made a complete set of duplicate keys which I always kept in a different place.

Talking of lost keys, recently, I came across an interesting news item. In England, in the city of Kent, the original key to the Kent Tower (the tower dates back to 1070 AD) had been long lost. ***Recently, the key was returned to the tower by post after forty seven years!*** Yes, that is correct, after forty seven years. The tower officials said it was really a mystery as to who returned it. They were so happy in getting back the original key that they offered a free membership to the Tower club in the hope that the mystery man would come forward.

While the above two incidents relate to keys that were lost and found, ***there are many keys that I am yet to find in the first place.***

For instance, even though I have heard about the key to happiness, the key to good health and the key to success in life, I am yet to get hold of any of these keys in the first place.

Meanwhile, the years have rolled by and the time to find out these keys is fast getting over.

One key that all of us seem to have lost is the key to happiness. Why do I say lost? Because, as children, most of us used to be happy. But somewhere along the way, we lost that key. Today, we find that there is unhappiness all around. In fact all studies indicate that ***even though humankind is at the zenith of technological prowess, people are unhappy as never before.*** Even today's children lose their happiness at an early age because their childhood and innocence are snatched away at a very early age.

Is it possible for a grown up to be happy at all? I feel it is possible. ***I think the first and foremost qualification needed to acquire the key to happiness is to develop a feeling of contentment.***

In the meantime, I just came across a bestselling book on Amazon 'How to be Happy'. I might just order that book because that book may really contain the key to happiness!

The Painting on the Wall

Recently, when I was travelling, I had to stay overnight in a hotel. As I arrived at the hotel, I noticed that the hotel looked beautiful with a large lawn on the side with an attractive garden. After I was shown to my room and my luggage delivered, I sat down and made myself comfortable. At night, I went down to the restaurant and had my dinner.

Later, as I was relaxing, I looked around the room. The room was dimly and beautifully lit. As I was taking in the scene, my eyes came to rest on a painting which was hung on the wall, illuminated by a small focused light.

I went closer and looked at the painting, trying to understand it. I could not really make out what the painting was about. To my ignorant, untrained eyes, it looked like a splattering of colours! As I sat back trying to understand the painting, my mind began to wander...

When and why did humans begin to paint? We know that cave and wall paintings have been a part of civilizations and of human history. But when were the first ever paintings made?

Recent archaeological discoveries show that the earliest cave paintings were made by the Neanderthals. The paintings date back about 65,000 years. Can anyone imagine how a painting could survive over such a long period? The paints of those days would have been made from leaves of shrubs and maybe some animal matter; but still they have survived all these ages, whereas the latest technologies of today cannot protect a painting for more than a few years!

When we think about great painters from the past, we normally think of painting as an art patronized by the rich and the famous. We know of painters of the royal courts of the world and think of painting as an art nurtured by royalty. We also read about paintings being sold in auctions for millions.

But in the days of the Neanderthals, one cannot imagine a life of luxury. The Neanderthals obviously struggled to stay alive each day, let alone indulge in painting as a luxury!

So then, why did the Neanderthals (or the early humans for that matter) paint? Well, in my opinion, what the discovery of the cave paintings implies is that ***painting is the manifestation of an innate urge. It is something by which a person expresses himself or herself, giving shape to his innermost yearnings and thoughts.***

That is one reason why psychologists attempt to understand our character traits by our interpretation of pictures.

When I was a student, I took a course in human psychology. The course was taught by the famous psychologist Rehana Ghadially. One day she brought a picture to class, displayed it and asked each of us to write a story based on the picture. That was my first exposure to the Thematic Apperception Test (TAT). Of course each one of us wrote entirely different stories; at the end of the class, she explained our character traits that led us to interpret the pictures in different ways and write different stories. I still treasure her analysis of my story - she concluded that I was a highly motivated individual.

Incidentally, paintings come in all sizes. The world's largest painting covers an area of 17,000 sq.ft; it is called the 'Journey of Humanity' and is an 'abstract' on canvas. This painting by British artist Sacha Jafri was made in 2020. It was sold for 62 million dollars! Sad to say, when I looked at an image of this painting, understanding this abstract art proved far beyond my capacity! At the other end of the spectrum, the world's smallest painting is less than one third of a human hair- a painting of a Monalisa by a team at Georgia University using a thermochemical nano technique.

Often we read about paintings being sold in auctions. Which is the world's most expensive painting ever? Well, the paintings by the great masters such as the Monalisa and the Last Supper are considered "priceless" and hence cannot be valued in terms of money. The costliest painting ever sold is Leonardo Da Vinci's "Salvatore Mundi" which went for a staggering 450 million US dollars!

But coming back to the painting in my hotel room - I must confess that even as I write this, I am still trying to understand this painting on the wall!

The Old Fool

Recently I had to attend a birthday party. It was in fact, the birthday party of my nephew's son - his seventh birthday. As you know, nowadays birthdays are celebrated in a big way, often in big hotels. So was it here too; the party was held in a star hotel. The stage was beautifully decorated with balloons and glittering colours. A big cake stood on one side of the stage. The birthday child and his parents were on the stage and stayed there most of the time. The child himself was dressed in a fine suit, one of those glitzy sherwani types that bridegrooms wear nowadays - obviously a birthday present from his parents.

After the prayers, the cake cutting ceremony took place. The father lifted up the child on his shoulders and helped him to cut the cake. The child then came into the gathering to distribute pieces of the cake. He carried a tray on which the pieces of the cake were placed.

It so happened that I was the oldest member in that gathering. So someone directed the little child to offer me the cake first. And the child came straight to me and offered me the tray. Now, I am old and my blood sugar levels are not exactly good; only the previous day, my doctor had admonished me on my sugar levels. The child now stood in front of me extending the tray; I was sorely tempted to take a piece of that creamy cake, but, quickly recollecting the doctor's advice, I decided to be strong. I declined the piece of cake.

Immediately, the child's face fell!

In all his childish innocence, he never could understand why I rebuffed his offer of the cake. He stood confused for a moment and then with a brave face, he moved on.

Almost immediately, I realised my blunder. I realised that I should have accepted the cake from the happy little child and blessed him. Later I could have given the cake to someone else. But, by now it was too late.

I had deeply hurt a small child; I had committed a grave blunder.

I realised that, sadly, this was getting to be a regular affair, committing blunders first and then regretting later. And as I got older, this was getting to be the norm.

Little wonder, they say "There is no fool like an old fool!"

As I sat there, regretting my action, my mind wandered back to another birthday party of a long time ago.

It is all so hazy nowadays, recollecting things from the long past. On some days, I find it quite easy. But on other days, it is indeed quite difficult; it is all a hazy mist and I have to pull out the images from the middle of the mist.

I was a small child and I was attending the birthday party of my best friend. I was nicely dressed in my best dress. After the cake cutting and the happy birthday songs, we were all standing around talking. At that time, my friend's mother brought sweets on a tray to offer us. Since I was nearest to her (or may be because I was her son's best friend), she offered me the tray first. Immediately, I put out both my hands and picked up as many sweets as I could. She graciously told me to take even more! I still remember the scene, she standing there with a beautiful smile on her gentle face. Greedily, I stuffed both my pockets with sweets and took still more sweets from the tray. Then she moved on. Almost immediately, I realised how bad my behaviour had been. I had let my greed get the better of me. Obviously, what I should have done was to take a few sweets and then thank her. Instead, I had greedily stuffed my pockets full with sweets.

I felt ashamed. What a blunder it was! But by now it was too late.

Unfortunately, actions are like words -you can never take them back.

Even today I shrink back in shame when I think about that incident.

Meanwhile in the party, all around me there was merry making. Everyone was chattering excitedly and the music was blaring. By now, the child and his family were back on stage, accepting presents. My wife had also purchased a present and we had to go on stage and hand it over.

As we stood on the steps to the stage, waiting our turn to get on the stage, my mind again wandered back into the hazy mist of my past.

I was a boy of seven or eight. It was my birthday. On birthdays, usually, there would be a prayer and my mother might make payasam in the evening. Sometimes I would get a birthday present. There would be some sweets at breakfast time too. And on this day, I waited on a chair in the kitchen after taking my breakfast, wondering what kind of present my mother would offer me.

My mother came to me and hugged me tenderly, praying softly.
And then she took out a boiled egg and gave me the boiled egg as a present! My mind was in a whirl. ***A boiled egg for a birthday present? What would I tell my friends?***
I was too young then to realise that presents do not matter, do not matter at all; what really matters is the love and affection that go behind a present. It took me a long time, in fact a very long time to realise that.
My mother is long gone. In all these years, though I have received many birthday presents, never did I receive a boiled egg again and never with so much love!
Meanwhile, we had reached the stage. When it was our turn, we handed over the present to the little child. As I held him close and blessed him, I handed over a packet of chocolates that my wife had thoughtfully purchased.
As the little boy's face lit up in delight, I realised that was the best present anyone could get!

The Tug of War

Onam is celebrated every year with gaiety and pomp by Keralites the world over. In our own residents association, all families celebrate the festival but the official Onam celebration function of the association usually takes place in the month following Onam. The celebration function is held on a Sunday evening and it is held in the school grounds near our house. There are games and sports followed by a formal meeting and dinner.

Usually, I skip the sports events and go in time for the formal meeting. But this time I decided to go early and watch the sports events. After a series of events like the musical chair and the spoon race came the tug of war. First, the women's events took place with everyone cheering on. Then came the men's tug of war, the day's final event.

As a senior citizen, I decided to behave my age and decided not to join the event. Even though many of the youngsters invited me to join, I politely declined and preferred to stand aside and watch. The men were split into two groups and the groups appeared to be evenly matched. The young boys (children) were evenly distributed into both the teams. All took their places on either side. As I stood aside and watched, I noted that one side had a towering pivot (as you know the pivotal position is usually taken by the strongest man in the team)–he was at least six feet three and massively built. His very presence in that team tilted the balance towards them. When the referee blew the whistle, both the teams gave it their all. They pulled and pulled. There was wild cheering by the onlookers. The side with the towering giant slowly and steadily began to pull over the other side amid wild cheers. Finally, they completely pulled over the other side and won the first round.

Watching the tug of war, I was reminded of a favourite story from my school days. Surely, you will be familiar with it too. An old farmer cultivated potatoes. One year, he had a very good crop. While all the plants grew well, one particular plant grew and grew. It stood towering over the other plants. Finally the time came for harvesting. The old man went around pulling out the plants one by one. When he came to the big plant, he pulled and pulled but it could not be pulled out. He called his wife and together they tried. One by one the three children of the family joined, stood one behind the other and pulled together but to no avail. Then the dog joined and then the cat, still they could not pull it out. A little mouse passing by saw the spectacle and it decided to help. It joined the effort and stood behind the cat pulling the cat's tail.

And lo and behold, the giant potato came loose and the whole group fell together in a heap!

You see, the little mouse had made all the difference!

Talking about the game of tug of war, it is a game that has existed from time immemorial. Various people trace its origin to Greece, China, India, Cambodia etc. Tug of war is so easy to play! And so many can take part - the only limitations are the length and strength of the rope. Many ancient countries promoted tug of war as an essential exercise for their armies.

Even today in many cultures, it is promoted on par with martial arts.

Incidentally, the world's largest tug of war takes place every year in Okinawa in Japan called Naha's tug of war. The rope used is 200 metres long and weighs more than forty tonnes! Hundreds of people make up the teams. Its origins can be traced back to the year 1450 AD.

While we talk about the game of tug of war, every moment there is a tug of war going on in our minds. The tug of war in our minds has no specific time or date. A tug of war can occur at any moment in our minds. Whenever two different desires occur or two different jobs need to be done there is a tug of war in our minds.

For example, one afternoon last week, my relatives decided to go to a super hit movie and they invited me to join them. At the same time an Asia Cup football match was scheduled on TV which I was planning for weeks to watch. A tug of war started between these two in my mind. ***You can say I was torn between two desires!*** Finally, the super hit movie won the day.

Recently I was standing in a bakery when a mother entered with her small child. The mother wanted to buy the child a piece of cake. The shelf of the shop had on it displayed not one, not two but at least five different types of cakes. Now in the child's mind there was a tug of war of a different kind- each cake pulled her mind in a different direction, I could see the struggle on her innocent face.

On a moral plane, in our minds, all the time, there is a tug of war between the forces of good and evil. *The forces of good (instilled in our mind from our childhood by parents, teachers and religion) have to constantly wage a tug of war against the forces of evil* ***(usually the much more desirable and attractive option!).***

While I was thinking about these things, on the ground, the tug of war teams changed sides and got ready for the second and final round. With the towering giant on one side, the weaker side demanded reinforcement. Old though I was, the team members insisted that I too join their team.

With the story of the little mouse fresh in my mind, I was only too happy to join their team and give my all.

What is in a Name

A few years ago, as I was driving along a highway, I was stopped by the red light at a junction. As I waited for the signal to change, I spent the time looking at the nearby shops. One shop caught my immediate attention: the reason - the name of the shop. In bright neon letters the name was prominently displayed: "**The No Name Shop!**" I was aghast - whoever would give such a name to a shop? And what about the customers, would anyone go to a shop with such a name; or without a name?

Ever since that day, whenever I have travelled on that route, I have always looked out for that shop; the shop's business has continued to grow over time and it is now a thriving shop with lots of customers.

That set me off thinking, ***does the name really matter? What is in a name after all?***

When we ask that question, we hear two answers: one, as the question itself implies, there is nothing in a name and hence it doesn't matter what the name is; the second answer to the question is "everything."

In our society, when we meet a stranger, we become curious to find out all about him. I have noticed that when two people meet, they may exchange information about their native place and other things but very soon they come to the critical question: ***what is your name one person asks slyly***. They ask the question in such a friendly manner, you may actually get misled into thinking that they have become fond of you and they want to call you by your name. Sadly, I have come to realize that the question is asked to "place" you; the underlying reasons may be actually to find out your religion and caste!

Now, coming to my own name, I admit that it is slightly uncommon! As a result, two things happen. One, people remember the name easily and two, my name is miss- spelt! In the south they think that I come from the north. Only last week, the lady in an office was quite surprised to know that I am from the south. Often I have to pay a price for my name- it is routinely misspelt. Recently, my gas agency computerised their records. The data entry people were smart but in a tearing hurry. When the new card came in, I was shocked to find it in the name of Joseph Pal. Now I have started the process to get my name corrected and prove to the agency that I am Jasper Lal and not Joseph Pal!

How do people name their children? Well, most often after consulting their astrologers and the elders in their families. Nowadays data banks are available on the net. Often people name their children on the spur of the moment. When Yuri Gagarin went into space, lakhs of children were named after him. Many of you will recall that a US satellite called "Sky lab" crashed through the atmosphere in the 80s. The world press created a huge suspense over when and where it would come down and how many people it would kill!

As the day approached, newspapers started countdown to doomsday and people were made to wait for the apocalypse. Finally, when it crashed down harmlessly into the ocean, everyone was relieved. So much so that one child who was born on that day was named "Skylab Singh" by his relieved parents. I wonder what the poor boy (who must be a man now) feels about it!

Incidentally, the longest name in the world is 747 characters long and belongs to Hubert Blaine Wolfeschlegelsteinhausenbergerdorff Sr. That gentleman lived in the USA and passed away in 1997. Obviously, his full name cannot be printed here because it may take half a page! The record for having the shortest individual name was set by J (born on December 19, 2013) of Chennai, Tamil Nadu. No one can find out his religion, caste and language from his name.

We all know that Elon Musk is the richest man in the world. We also know that he appears to be slightly quirky at times! In 2020, when Elon Musk's son was born, he and his girlfriend named their son "**X Æ A-Xii**"! Yes, it is true, you can verify from the net. Each letter is supposed to have a meaning too: Æ stands for Artificial Intelligence, Xii stands for the number of his favourite aircraft and so on.

Now that perhaps is the ultimate answer to the question what is in a name!

The Prisoner

One of the super hit movies of the year 2023 was "The Prisoner" starring a South superstar.

Even though I am not a regular moviegoer, I still keep in touch. So I knew that the reviews of the film were uniformly good. They all raved about the superstar's performance. The first day's collection in the theatres broke many records. Even after a month, the film was still running to packed houses. Taken in by all the euphoria, I decided not to miss out on a good thing and decided to watch the film.

But nothing that I read in the reviews had prepared me for the film - blood flowed like water throughout the three hours. Let me tell you about a few scenes- a scene that was particularly revolting showed the superstar at his dining table along with his wife. Just then a group of villains attacked through the windows and doors. Of course, they were all shot or hacked to death and the bodies piled up on the dining table, blood splattering the face of his wife. The wife recoiled in horror but the superstar nonchalantly offered her a tissue to wipe away the blood and perhaps continue eating!

Later on in the movie, it turned out that the superstar had been a prison warden, where he maintained ironclad discipline. One day, during the morning drill, one convict was caught making a bit of mischief; the result - the superstar had the convict's ear chopped off and displayed for all of us to see in a gory close up! At the end of the three hours, I managed to stagger out of the theatre. I was numb and dazed. I thought perhaps a strong coffee might renew my spirits. I managed to walk to the lift, reach the coffee shop on the top floor and order a hot cup of strong coffee. The strong coffee steadied me. Now I could again think clearly.

I came down, crossed the road and took a bus to my part of the city. By now it was evening. I got down from the bus and started walking. The route took me along the main road near an area where many mobile eatery vans did business. That day too, many eatery vans were doing brisk business. One particular van caught my attention - it had the red and white nameplate of a government vehicle. On getting closer, I realised that it was a vehicle of the prison department. There was a good crowd surrounding the van. Men from the vehicle were selling food items prepared by prison inmates - a chapatti and chicken combo made by the prison inmates was selling like hotcakes.

It occurred to me that the money earned by the sales must be going to help various welfare initiatives for the inmates. While in general prisoners have a tough time, various initiatives are launched by governments for prisoner welfare. So much so that, it is alleged that the latest reforms effectively dilute the severity of prison terms.

At the end of it all, there is no doubt that many prisoners come out of prison reformed while many others come out as hardened criminals!

While thinking about prisons, I realise that each one of us are living in prisons of our own.

These prisons that we live in are invisible.
Basically there are two types of prisons that we live in: one made by society and the other made by each one of us.
Society makes a rigid set of rules that we have to live by. It is impossible to escape this prison. These rules have evolved over thousands of years and now they have become an invisible prison. Society tells you how to dress, how to maintain decor, how to behave with other people. How men and women should interact and behave. How they should dress. Occasionally, it even tells you what to eat and dictates how you should think! Right from a very young age, society exerts its power over you. Young people who try to escape this prison are labelled rebels! There are a few rebels who manage to break free but for the majority, the rebellion dies down gradually. Often, a rebel may become an enforcer of the rules in her or his old age. A simple example would be a typical mother in law – mothers in law start out as rebellious young brides and end up as shrewish mothers in law in their old age!
There is no escape at all from this prison as long as you live and this prison is common to all humans in a society.
But there is yet another invisible prison in which we live - this one is built by each one of us. This prison varies from person to person. ***This prison basically is a set of thought patterns that enmesh us, muzzle us and control us.*** Often, this prison takes the form of an inner voice. Whenever you want to do something that may deviate from your routine, this voice tells you that you cannot do it, that you will bungle it. It keeps you on a tight leash like a dog on a chain. This prison creates a fear of failure and even a fear of success- it can basically render us immobilised and incapable!

But how did we build this prison around us?
We built this prison in our youth using various inputs: warnings by our elders when we were children, messages from our friends that told us that we were good at something or no good at anything, random occurrences in which people reacted to our behaviour etc.
Is it possible to escape from this prison which each one of us has built around us? Yes, but it takes a lot of patience, understanding, effort and hard work of course.
In the meantime, as I was about to pass by the mobile prison eatery, the men inside called out to me to buy something. I decided to buy a combination of chapattis and hot curry. Indeed, it would be a delicious dinner after the ordeal of the day!

Age could Bend him but not Break him

Whenever I have to catch a flight, I always try to reach the airport quite early. Reaching early gives one plenty of time; you can sit back with a book and catch up on the reading. Of course, in order to read, you have to try to sit as far away from the crowd as possible. Occasionally, you may also have to pretend that you did not see a friend coming! If you get bored with the book, you can always sit back and observe the goings-on.

So it was the other day, I had reached the airport very early and was observing the goings-on. There were people of different ages, sizes and shapes. Whole families together, a large number of young couples, some mothers with wailing small babies and so on. Amongst all this ruckus, one elderly gentleman caught my attention - he was tall, maybe six feet two and elegantly dressed. He had on white trousers and a grey overcoat. He was walking with the aid of a cane and his back was bent. ***Watching him cross the floor, a thought flashed through my mind - "age could bend him, but not break him."*** Slowly, the gentleman crossed the floor and vanished from my sight, but the thought stayed with me throughout the day.

Every day, do we not come across people who are bent by age and life but who continue to fight and whom life is not able to break?

As one ages, the challenges to be faced in life remain the same as in our younger days or they may be even more than before - but the resources to meet the challenges are less. Less in terms of health, money, social standing and literally in terms of every parameter. It is a myth to say that old age is like old wine, perhaps also wrong to say that old age is a time for relaxation. ***In our country, for 90% of the aged, old age is a time of endless challenges, a time when they are forced to work to survive.*** That is the time when life tries to bend them and break them.

I recall an aged couple from my young days. The husband was blind, the frail wife used to support him; she was like his walking stick. Together, they went from house to house seeking alms, never ill tempered, always accepting their fate. In the evenings, they went back to a thatched hut, a small shack about five feet size to sleep. This shack they had built on to the wall of a prominent building in the town, at an important junction. Of course, this hut adjoining the important building was an eyesore. They were warned many times to go away. But where could such a couple go? Who would give them a place? It was a struggle just staying alive, let alone moving away from that place and setting up a new hut.

And then one day, a terrible thing happened. The town woke up to the news that their hut had burned down during the night - with both of them inside. Only their charred remains were found inside. Was it that the shack caught fire accidentally or was it by design***? Did the couple decide to end it all or did someone else take that decision? No one will ever know.*** In a few days, all traces of the hut disappeared as the place was cleaned up. I did absolutely nothing about the whole thing, no one else did anything either - maybe powerful people were involved! Even though this happened such a long time ago, when I think about it, a feeling of guilt, helplessness and uneasiness still persists in my mind.

Do we all not come across such heart rending incidents? Don't we all look away? Of course we console ourselves that there is nothing much that an individual can do.

The other day as I was travelling by road, l took a tea break. I parked my car on the side of a restaurant and had tea and snacks. Just as I came out of the restaurant, an elderly man accosted me, carrying a bundle of lottery tickets. As I bought a ticket and started talking to him, I noticed that he was bent with age. It turned out that he was in his late eighties! As I expressed my unabashed admiration to him for earning his own living at his age, we started talking and it turned out that not only was he earning his own living, he was supporting others too. Now, here was a man whom age could not break.

Every day, we come across many people who are bent by age and life but who continue to fight and whom age and life are not able to break - the elderly vegetable seller pushing his cart just as we come out of the supermarket after buying "fresh" vegetables; the elderly auto driver with the trembling hands who struggles to keep up with the traffic and has to listen to abuses at the traffic junction; the bent old lady with the thick glasses at a traffic signal knocking on our window and trying to sell a pen. The list is endless.

These are the "people who are bent by life and age but who do not allow age or life to break them." The least we can do is to appreciate them and stand by them, at least when circumstances permit - when we can lend a helping hand at no great cost.

Happy Days are here Again

Everyone loves a good soft drink. Not too long ago, they were known as "cool drinks", I think mainly because they were served cold and also because it was "cool" to drink them. During my youth, the famous cool drinks of the era were Fanta, Limca, Thumbs-up, Campa Cola, 7up etc. But the undisputed leader was Thumbs Up (later on Thumsup) by biscuit major Parle. Thumsup remained the market leader throughout the late seventies and eighties till the early nineties when it was bought over by Coca Cola.

There was a famous advertisement for Thumsup - the song "happy days are here again." This commercial used to appear regularly during breaks in TV shows and also during film shows in theatres. The commercial showed a group of happy trendy young people drinking the fizzy Thumsup, a young man surrounded by a bevy of beautiful, somewhat scantily clad young women. The message of the song was clear - if you drank Thumsup, happiness came to you - probably it came searching for you.

Without doubt the main reason for Thumsup winning the market was the promise of happy days coming back to you along with your youth. Now, I ***had youth on my side but not the happiness seen in the video and definitely no young woman looked at me twice!*** So, I decided to try out Thumsup.

In fact, I drank gallons of Thumsup in the hope that I would get happiness and the women would come. I drank Thumsup standing in front of shops and standing on my balcony. But neither happiness nor the women came – instead, what came was a loss of appetite and sickness. Finally, I was dragged to the doctor. The doctor was scathing in his pronouncement, "You fool, who told you that drinking Thumsup will bring happiness?" Thus ended my search for happiness in my youth.

Originally, "happy days are here again" was a promise first made in the US during their general election in the year 1932 by the then opposition. The year 1929 had been the darkest year in American history. It was the year of the greatest stock market crash till date, resulting in the great depression of the 1930s. Millions lost their livelihood and their lives too! So, when the next presidential election came up in 1932, the opposition came up with the song - happy days are here again. Just look at the words - happy days are here again- meaning happy days were there earlier, they were taken away and will now come back to you again. No need to say, it was a winning song and the opposition won the election.

In the run up to the last general election in our state, I found one of the most soothing and comforting advertisements ever, displayed all over the state; it simply promised - "everything will become alright." Your part was simple: you only had to vote for one party, then, everything would become alright. It sounded so soothing to know that your vote would make everything alright!

But coming back to happy days, happy days are promised not only by soft drink makers, but, by many others, especially by flat builders. A few months ago, during one of my evening strolls, I found that a big hoarding had come up at a major junction put up by a flat builder - ***if you bought one of their flats, you could live happily ever after!*** Within a few days, I found that the same hoarding had come up at many locations in the city. That convinced me that this was the key to my happiness. The advertisement carried a contact number. I phoned the number secretly. The voice at the other end was welcoming and convincing. When I enquired about the cost of the flat, I found that it cost a fortune. Undeterred, I decided to buy one of their flats.

They say that men become wise with age. But there is also another saying – there is no fool like an old fool!

So to get happiness, in my old age, I was convinced that I had to buy one of their flats, spending a fortune. I planned to take a huge loan, sell everything I owned and then buy the flat and happiness.

I did not tell anything to my wife, I went about it quietly and secretively. Somehow she grew suspicious. One day, when I was going out with all my documents, she caught me red handed. Thus ended my quest for happiness in my old age.

I think by now you have understood the power of advertisements over my life. Being a simple person, I completely believed whatever the advertisements told. So after a lot of thinking, I decided not to even look at advertisements. I have stuck to my decision ever since.

But last week I came across a wonderful new advertisement. It was for a two wheeler by one of the top Indian companies - it was a poster of a handsome young man driving a scooter; but what really caught my attention was the caption under the picture - ***it said the two wheeler "runs on respect!"***

I was thrilled, to put it simply. ***Just imagine, this two wheeler does not need petrol or gas, it does not need a battery; all that it needs is respect! What a wonderful vehicle it must be***. I was so excited, the whole night and the next day I spent thinking only about it.

Now, If you still wonder how a two wheeler can run on respect alone, please think about it carefully, examine all technical possibilities and do consult the experts- but ***in the meantime, let me rush and do my booking for this magical two wheeler- before it sells out!***

How Are You?

It is such a simple question - "how are you?"
When we meet someone on the road or in a get together we exchange pleasantries; we may shake hands, curtsy to each other, smile , nod and so on. But sooner rather than later, we are likely to ask the question "How are you?"
In our culture, we have an aversion to giving an honest straightforward answer to this question. One reason is that, from childhood we are taught to be not exuberant and instead give sober and very modest answers. Another reason is the belief that telling another person that you are doing well bodes ill for your future well-being.
So the common answers that one gets would be words to the effect: I am getting along, I am not too bad, I am managing to survive etc. Listening to these answers, one would get the feeling that the person was struggling to stay alive!
Recently, I made the mistake of asking this question to a friend I met after a long time. Even though I had not met him for quite some time, I was well aware of his well-being. In fact, I was aware that he was doing well both at a personal and official level. But when I asked him the question, he immediately launched into a long drawn answer fully detailing all his recent "misfortunes", all the time directly looking into my eyes; I knew I was trapped and there was no way to escape. I had to stand

patiently and show interest till another friend came along and joined us, when I could make good my escape.

There are other occasions such as when you meet someone who is genuinely going through troubled times. This person may respond in different ways when you ask him the question– sometimes, he may make light of his troubles and put up a cheerful front. On the other hand, he may decide to share his troubles with you and sometimes may seek your advice too.

Because of all these possibilities, whenever I meet someone, I am in a dilemma –should I ask him the question or not.

Most people visit a place of worship at least one day a week. I too am in the habit of visiting a church and praying one day a week. When you visit a place of worship, you will notice that there are many people who sit around these places begging for alms. You will find that some of them are genuinely deserving of our sympathy - they may be really disabled and with no other means of earning a livelihood.

Recently, I came across one such person. There is a church we visit every week. Outside this church, sitting quite apart from the noisy alms seekers, I noticed one young man; he was probably in his early thirties – but he could barely move without help. Apparently, he was disabled from birth. I noticed that he had a quiet, smiling face. I felt compelled to talk to him and I asked him about himself, where he was from and so on. A slight acquaintance developed between us. Every time I came out of the church I would talk to him.

And then I did not see him for quite a few weeks. I surmised that probably, his health was going through a bad phase. Maybe he was undergoing treatment somewhere. Every week I kept looking for him.

Last week, when I went to the church, I found him sitting in his regular place.

As I approached him, I noticed that he looked wan; his complexion was pale and apparently, he was in pain; he had been sitting in the hot sun since morning.

Without thinking, I asked him the question, "How are you?"

He answered with a smile, **"I am fine sir!"**

As I gave him some money and turned away from him, tears filled my eyes - I was strangely moved. ***Here was a man who was crippled, who was suffering, who was helpless and yet, he was telling me with a smile "I am fine sir!"***

Nowadays, I resist the temptation to ask this question to anyone. Instead, I say things like "I hope things are alright," "I hope you are managing at your end;" often I start telling about myself first, hoping the other person will respond in a similar fashion ***if he so wishes.***

After all, who knows what he is going through?

Changing Times

Some time ago, I came across interesting news. A woman was being released from prison after 53 years. The woman was Leslie Van Houten, a follower of the infamous American cult leader Charles Manson. Charles Manson established a cult called "the family" in the 1960s. The "family" carried out nine murders of innocent people including that of actress Sharon Tate (who was nine months pregnant at that time). Leslie Van Houten was convicted for her part in two murders. She was 19 years old at that time.

Recently when she was released on parole, she was 73 years old, having spent 53 years in prison.

She entered prison as a 19 year old teenager who barely knew the world. Last month she entered a world she did not know at all, it had changed so much in the 53 years.

How can this woman adjust to the strange new world? Everything will be so different! In fact, ***"She has to actually re-learn to live!"***

Reading about this lady reminded me of a story that we all read in school - the story of Rip Van Winkle.

Rip Van Winkle was a farmer. One day he went into the mountains where he met a few strange men from his native land. The men played strange instruments. He started drinking with them, getting fully drunk. Finally, he passed out.

When he woke up, it was a sunny day. None of the strange men were around. Slowly he made his way to his village - everyone and everything was different. ***He had been asleep for 20 long years!***

If Rip Van Winkle woke up after twenty years, this woman Leslie was waking up and entering the real world after fifty three years.

Recently, I visited a relative's house after about fifteen years. I had to board a bus and travel for a few hours to reach the place. In my mind, I had a clear image of what that place would look like - an image formed 15 years ago. But today, when I got off the bus, I could not get a bearing at all. Not even one building remained the same. Forget the buildings, the roads were different, the trees had all disappeared, there was a shopping complex where a pond had been. The shops were different. There was not one person on the road who looked familiar!

If this is the change in fifteen years, can you imagine how much would change in fifty years?

Our dress, our hair style, our language have all changed. The structure of the family has undergone a great change. Respect for age and elders has all but disappeared. ***Chivalry is dead.***

In the last fifty years, communication has become instantaneous. Fifty years ago, we sent home letters by post and got back the answer after two or three weeks. ***But today communication travels faster than thought.***

In the last 50 years, mother earth has been brought to her knees. Thousands of species have become extinct including insects and birds. When you woke up 50 years ago, you heard birds singing. Gone are those days. Today to hear a bird sing, either you search and listen on the internet or you may have to go to a zoo.

Cities have become concrete and glass jungles with huge populations. There are crowds everywhere. The world is a much hotter place today. It is also much more polluted.

Travel has changed. Air travel is much more common. The automobiles of fifty years ago are today classified as vintage. Healthcare is definitely one that has changed. The average life expectancy has definitely gone up. Sadly the cost of medical support has also gone up steeply.

While things around us have changed, what has not changed is what lies within us.

Our feelings of love and hate, our prejudices – perhaps these are the things that will never change!

The Bermuda Triangle in my Home

The Bermuda Triangle is a triangular area in the North Atlantic Ocean extending over 2,00,000 sq.km. Legend has it that many ships and aircraft have mysteriously disappeared while in the vicinity of the Bermuda Triangle. These incidents are reported from the mid nineteenth century to the later part of the twentieth century but mainly in the mid twentieth century. A number of books have been written on the Bermuda Triangle. Over the years, many explanations have been attempted. Many claim there is nothing mysterious and it is only hype. They claim that each occurrence is logically explained. But the faithful believe differently and for them it is a mystery like no other. Explanations that have been proffered include: the presence of paranormal activity, UFO related, undersea currents, disturbance in the earth's magnetic field and so on. ***But the one I found most interesting was that of time warping ie, time slows down in the area!***

Over the years the Bermuda Triangle has come to denote any area where there are mysterious occurrences.

Now you may be wondering why I bring up the topic of the Bermuda Triangle. You may also wonder how I learned so much about it. Let me tell you all about it.

You see, ***there is a small area in my house where there are mysterious happenings. Essentially, time seems to slow down***

in the area. I will tell you how I noticed it. There was a wall clock of a reputed brand which used to be on our guest room wall. One day I decided to shift that clock to our work area (henceforth denoted Bermuda Triangle area). But once I mounted the clock in its new position, it immediately began to slow down. I thought perhaps, the battery needed to be changed. So I put a new battery on the clock, but still the clock continued to slow down. Not one to give up without a fight, I took the clock to our neighbourhood watch and clock repair man. After examining the clock thoroughly, he said that the clock mechanism had to be changed. I agreed and the mechanism itself was changed. I brought back the clock and mounted it back on the wall. The next day morning when I checked, the clock was back to its tricks - it had slowed down by an hour.

Now this really upset me.

I decided to make another effort. I took down the main clock from our front room and put it up at the mystery location. I was quite sure this clock would run normally. Imagine my shock when I checked on it the next day - it had slowed down by an hour!

Really puzzled by now, I shifted the clock back to its original location and found that it was running normally.

Something mysterious was indeed going on. In order to get to the bottom of the business, I started searching the net about time slowing down - ***that is when I discovered all about the Bermuda Triangle! I was now convinced that a similar phenomenon was at work in my home.***

Just when I was brooding about this whole business, I came across an interesting post on WhatsApp. It is now viral in

WhatsApp. You might have seen it too. It was about Flight 513, a commercial airliner operated by Santiago Airlines that departed from Aachen, Germany, on September 4, 1954, with 88 passengers and four crew members on board. The aircraft was headed towards Porto Alegre, Brazil. The plane disappeared without a trace soon after take-off, causing despair and confusion among relatives of the passengers, crew and the aviation industry. Despite relentless search and rescue efforts, no wreckage or any sign of the aircraft was found.

On October 12, 1989, 35 years after its disappearance, the plane suddenly reappeared, landing perfectly at Porto Alegre's airport, stunning air traffic controllers. ***When the security team checked the plane, they found the haunting sight of the skeletal remains of all 92 people in their seats with the pilot still clutching the controls. There were accompanying photos of the skeletons too, just in case you did not believe!***

The narrator further stated that the most widely held explanation behind Santiago Flight 513 was the wormhole theory, claiming that the flight most probably would have entered a "time hole," which meant the plane travelled through time. ***Hence there was a slowing down of time!*** According to the narrator, the only question that remained was who piloted the plane during the landing.

By now, my mind was in a daze. I had to do something urgently! I began to consult all and sundry. I am indeed thankful that a lot of advice came in.

Based on all the advice, now I am on my way to consult a well-known Vaasthu expert. I have little doubt that the problem lay in the fact that I had not consulted a Vaasthu expert when I built my house.

I will definitely rectify my mistake now!

The Pick Pocket

One day last week, I was walking along a busy main road. I had to go to the bus stand and catch a bus out of the city. It was a hot and humid day and I was sweating profusely. I decided to stop at a roadside shop just before the junction and have a glass of cold fresh fruit juice. The shop offered cold apple juice, guava juice and pineapple juice. Just as I finished ordering a fresh apple juice, I heard loud voices nearby.

Looking towards the junction, I saw that a crowd had collected. On venturing closer, I saw that the crowd was thrashing a man in a red shirt. The man was on his knees and begging with folded hands but a few in the crowd would not let up - they continued to kick him and beat him with sticks. I played it safe and went back to my juice stall. Very soon a police jeep came and took the man away.

When I asked the dispersing people what had happened, they said the man had been caught pickpocketing and had been meted out instant justice!

As I stood in the shelter of the shop waiting for my fruit juice to get ready, my mind wandered back to a day five decades ago when my pocket was picked for the first time.

I was on a crowded local train in Bombay. It was the first time that I was travelling on a Bombay local. There were two main suburban railway lines running through Bombay which were the city's life lines - the central and the western. The central line was far more crowded than the western and I was travelling on a central line local.

When the train halted at the next stop, a crowd of people got onto the train - which was already overflowing with people. I was caught right in the middle of this surge. ***The mass of people inside the crowd now moved as a single unit, nothing could move inside that mass itself.*** I felt that my bones were about to be crushed. I could hardly breathe! I could neither move my hands nor my legs. When the train halted at the next stop and disgorged the crowd, I too was pulled along onto the platform. I clung on to the door handle and managed to pull myself back in time before the train started again.

Finally, I arrived at my stop, got off the train and hobbled off to my room. My whole body was in pain. I thought I would take a hot cup of tea at the corner tea stall near my room. When I put my hand into my pocket to take out my purse, to my utter surprise, my hand went right through! ***There was no purse and there was no more a pocket!***

Shocked, I ran to my room. On taking off my trousers, I found a gaping hole where my pocket had been. On looking closer, I saw that the pocket had been neatly cut, probably with a sharp blade by skilled hands! When did the pickpocket cut open my pocket? As I pondered over that, I realised the pickpocket must have carried out his job when I was caught in the bone crushing crowd. To add to my woes, I realised that my ID card had been inside my purse and that was lost too.

Two weeks after this incident, our postman called on me one day and handed over an envelope. On cutting open the envelope what did I find but my ID card! There was a small piece of paper in the same envelope and something was typed on that paper. Eagerly I read it. In bold letters it was typed "Be more careful with your ID card." It was signed (typed) "XXX" at the bottom.

To this day I wonder who sent me back my ID card.

Was it the pickpocket himself who had a gentle heart hidden away deep inside him? On second thought, the man after going through my purse could have pocketed the money and thrown away the ID card. Perhaps some Good Samaritan picked it up from the floor and mailed it to me. But then why did he sign it as XXX?

I will never know.

As the days rolled by, gradually, I learned the tricks of travelling in the crowded Bombay local trains and taking care of my ID card as advised by the pickpocket.

Talking of pickpockets, while there have been many master pickpockets in history, the most famous appears to be a gentleman named Apollo Robbins, a pickpocket from the USA. His greatest feat was when he picked the pocket of a secret service agent accompanying former US President Jimmy Carter. He managed to remove the president's car keys from the secret agent! After his feat became known, major security agencies and police departments approached him to learn his tricks. Known as the gentleman thief, today he is a well-known celebrity on TV.

In the meantime, my cold apple juice was ready. The sharp cold taste of the juice provided a comfortable relief to the hot and humid day!

The Conman

Last month, newspapers reported the passing of one Mr Dhani Ram Mittal. I had not really heard about this gentleman and so tried to find out how this gentleman became famous. Well, it turned out that he was one of the country's top conmen, that is how! As a young man, while employed as a clerk with law firms, he forged certificates and managed to become a railway station master. In the meantime, he started stealing cars from the courtyard to overcome his boredom. In all, he is believed to have stolen about a thousand cars. But his major claim to fame was when he forged papers and took on the identity of a magistrate. ***Using this fake identity, he ordered the release of a number of prisoners serving long prison terms!*** And he repeated this feat a number of times. That is how he acquired his fame and name! Mind you, all of his criminal activity was just for the thrill of it. ***Here was a conman, true to his art for the sake of the art!***

"Mr Natwarlal" was a 1979 movie starring Amitabh Bachchan and Rekha in the lead roles. I am sure many of you would have watched the movie. The film was a super hit. There were a number of fabulous songs in the movie including one sung by Amitabh himself (the first time Amitabh sang his own song onscreen). The inspiration behind the movie was India's most famous conman Natwarlal.

Natwarlal started off early in life by forging his neighbour's cheque and discovered that he had a special gift for forging documents and cheques. He was arrested any number of times and spent time in prison, often escaping using his ingenuity. There was a particular instance when he walked out of prison in a police uniform that was smuggled into his prison room and he was saluted by the constables on duty as he walked out! Natwarlal's life is surrounded by many myths about his exploits. The most famous ones relate to how he sold off the Taj Mahal and the parliament buildings. In his own village, he was a Robin Hood. He conned only the rich and spent a lot of money helping the poor. It is believed he passed away in 2009.

A few years ago, news came about conmen attempting to sell a star hotel in Chennai. The conmen contacted a firm in Kerala with an offer to sell a star hotel. They claimed that they wanted to clear their debts by selling off their hotel. They then hired a room in the same hotel and booked another room for the buyers. When the buyers arrived, they took them around the hotel and showed them the hotel. Then, they boldly started negotiations in the hotel lobby itself. Unfortunately for them, one hotel staffer grew suspicious and alerted the hotel management who called in the police!

Victor Lustig is the famous conman who managed to sell the Eiffel Tower, not once but twice! He pulled off the scam when the tower was in a state of disrepair and there was no funding to maintain it. Posing as a government official, he called a meeting of the city's scrap dealers and convinced them that the government was selling off the tower as scrap! He identified the most gullible one in the group, worked on him and sold him the deal. Once he collected a good sum of money as an advance, he fled to Austria. Later, when he attempted the same with another group, the police got wind of it and he fled to America.

Closer home, we had a famous conman in Kerala who conned quite a few celebrities. He preyed only on the rich and the famous. He passed off local items as antiques and could convince everyone with his glib tongue. One of the best jobs that he pulled was passing off a walking stick as Moses's staff which Moses had used to part the Red Sea!

Conmen come in all guises. From money investment schemes to selling fake medicines to palming off useless things on hapless customers.

Of course, we all get a good laugh when we look at the people who get fooled. But what about us? Have you ever been conned?

Let me confess, in my own case, I have been duped any number of times by conmen.

Back in the nineties, at the height of the stock market boom, a number of investment schemes came in the market to feed on the gullible. I for once, fell for all of them! I recall, one scheme was for setting up a goat farm. Another one as I recall was floated for a farm growing tamarind trees! Yet another one was for a teak farm. All these schemes promised phenomenal returns. Without fail, I invested in all of them. The conmen in all these cases collected my hard earned money and then disappeared without a trace!

Over the years, I have prided myself that I can spot a conman when I see one. A few months ago, I had to urgently travel from Bombay by train; I had no reservation. As I was wandering on the platform looking into the crowded compartments wondering what to do, a very kind gentleman approached me; he looked vaguely familiar too. Luckily for me, this gentleman was also in the same plight. But fortunately, he knew whom to contact and how to get a confirmed seat. Happy with the kind Good Samaritan, I gave him the money for the ticket and a good extra amount needed to bribe whoever it was. As he rushed off to get our tickets, I was really happy that I could find the right man to help me. I waited for him to come back with the tickets for a long time. But then I never saw him again!

So, my friends, the next time someone offers to help you out of the way, keep your senses wide open. You never know when a conman comes!

About the Author

Jasper Lal Chith is a graduate of IIT Bombay and a postgraduate of IIT Madras. He worked in the Indian Space Research Organisation (ISRO) for three decades and a half. He is an acclaimed expert in Rocket Propulsion and has contributed to the development of ISRO launch vehicles. He lives in Trivandrum, India.